THREE WEDDINGS AND A BABY

HEART FALLS VIGNETTE COLLECTION: VOL. 1

VIVIAN AREND

Three Weddings and a Baby
Copyright © 2020 by Arend Publishing Inc.
ISBN: 9781989507223
Edited by Manuela Velasco
Cover Design © Damonza
Proofed by Angie Ramey & Linda Levy

MESSAGE FROM VIVIAN

After the story is done, *their* stories go on.

One of the great parts of writing a long family saga is getting to revisit characters who have already hit their happily-ever-after.

The first three stories in this collection are the weddings of the couples from *The Stones of Hearts Falls* series. These are NOT full length stories. More a "moment in their lives". The vignettes have appeared before in newsletters, and they're available for free on my website, but I've placed them here for your convenience to read on your device.

But the baby part in the title? That's brand new!

I simply had to write a novella for Josiah Ryder and Lisa Coleman (The Cowgirl's Forever Love) to go with this collection. As it turns out... Yup! There are big changes in store for the Heart Falls veterinarian and our favourite *shenanigan* coordinator. Of course, Ollie the terrier is also a huge part of this story. She says to tell you *bark, bark, bark*!

~

CHECK the intros first to see where the individual stories fit into the full series reading order if you want to avoid spoilers for books you haven't yet read! There's a reading order on the next page if you want to make sure you've read all the books so far. I've jumped around a little between series, so if you've missed any, now's the time to catch up!

I hope these stories make you smile.

With love from me and your friends in Heart Falls.

***You'll see what Ollie says at the conclusion of Oh Baby!*

HEART FALLS SERIES CHRONOLOGICAL READING ORDER

A Rancher's Heart (The Stones of Heart Falls, Book 1)

Surprised at Bootstomp Point (Heart Falls Vignette Collection Vol.1)

A Rancher's Song (The Stones of Heart Falls, Book 2)

A Firefighter's Christmas Gift (Holidays in Heart Falls, Book 1)

A Rancher's Bride (The Stones of Heart Falls, Book 3)

Heartfelt at Heart Falls (Heart Falls Vignette Collection Vol.1)

The Cowgirl's Forever Love (The Colemans of Heart Falls, Book 1)

A Wild Horse Wedding (Heart Falls Vignette Collection Vol.1)

The Cowgirl's Secret Love (The Colemans of Heart Falls, Book 2)

The Cowgirl's Chosen Love (The Colemans of Heart Falls, Book 3)

A Soldier's Christmas Wish (Holidays in Heart Falls, Book 2)

Oh, Baby! (Heart Falls Vignette Collection Vol.1)

A Hero's Christmas Hope (Holidays in Heart Falls, Book 3)

Coming soon:

A Rancher's Love (The Stones of Heart Falls, Book 4)

PART I

SURPRISED AT BOOTSTOMP POINT

Surprising Tamara isn't the easiest at the best of times, but Caleb is determined to make this special event happen without her coordinating it. With help from his oldest daughter, and a return visit to a memorable meeting spot, it's time for Tamara to truly become a part of the Stone family.

Timeline: This scene takes place on the first day of summer after **A Rancher's Heart** and before **A Rancher's Song.**

CALEB

June 21st, Silver Stone ranch

There weren't many things that scared Caleb Stone. Not many things that he obsessed over or worried about. Not unless he got to thinking about his family.

When it came to them, he spent time and energy every day to make sure things were going well. And every day he was happy to count his blessings as his world got richer and happier because he had them with him.

Stood to reason he should do something to add to *their* happiness if he could.

His little girls, Sasha and Emma, were his heart stones. The rest of his family—whom he'd raised—was all tangled up around him as well, sometimes literally.

Like as he pushed through the barn doors and was nearly flattened by his brother Dustin, who was moving at a near run in the opposite direction.

"Watch where you're going," Caleb grumbled.

"Sorry. Tamara texted and asked if I could grab something from town for her."

Caleb resisted the urge to roll his eyes like his oldest daughter had a tendency to do. "Finished work already?"

Dustin paused, looking a little guilty. "I promise I'll get back to it and finish up before I stop for the night."

Caleb waved a hand at him. The hero worship Dustin had for Tamara was only getting stronger, but in this case, her asking for a favour was a good thing.

It meant they wouldn't accidentally have his little brother tagging along on what he was planning as a small family outing with just him, Tamara, and the girls.

"Go on. Stop at the post office and check if there's anything for us as well."

"Sure thing, boss," Dustin offered as he took off at a brisk walk, trying to look casual.

Caleb shook his head as he went back into the barn and saddled up their horses, whistling as he worked, pretty sure he was about to make at least three people very happy.

Four, if he included himself. Not a bad idea on the first day of summer.

"If you get much cheerier, the horses might complain." His brother Luke leaned over the edge of the pen where Caleb had gone to grab the horse Sasha had claimed as her own.

"Because horses don't like people to be happy around them?"

Luke grabbed a saddle blanket and laid it over Firecracker's back. "Horses like stability, and you're definitely a whole lot perkier than you were a year ago."

Caleb wasn't going to argue. "I didn't have Tamara in my life a year ago."

Luke gave his shoulder a solid pat of approval. "Well then, I guess the horses are just going to have to get used to you not being a grumpy bastard."

"Let's not push it too far. How about a *less* grumpy bastard?" Caleb offered his brother a grin. "I don't want to promise too much."

"Under promise, over deliver. Best sales system ever." Luke checked his watch. "Walker said he'd call when he was done riding today with an update on his standings. I'll stop by later to catch you up."

"I'm taking Tamara and the girls out for supper, and then we're dropping them at a friend's house for a sleepover."

Luke raised a brow. "Okay. I got the message. I will *not* be stopping by the house tonight for a visit."

"Smart man."

Caleb went back to saddling the horses, taking a quick peek at his own watch. He didn't want to be late. Not for this, and with three women to wrangle without letting them know he had an agenda, he had to get moving.

Luckily, it had turned out to be a beautiful day, and the horses were pleased as punch to follow him to the railing outside the house where he tied them up. He took the steps onto the porch with his feet barely touching the ground.

Sasha opened the door. "Mommy is getting dressed," she whispered.

"Did you give her my present?"

Sasha nodded, happiness dancing in her eyes. "She looks pretty."

"Your mom looks pretty in everything." He bent down and kissed Sasha before pressing a finger to her lips. He hadn't told Emma the secret, but Sasha he could trust to keep her mouth shut, and he'd needed a co-conspirator.

It had pleased his oldest girl so much to be told the secret. And that was another part of family—growing in new ways. As strange as it seemed to discover he no longer had toddlers but small people who had definite ideas and opinions of their own.

Emma came around the corner, stomping her feet in her new cowboy boots. "They feel funny," she complained.

He reached down and helped her pull up her socks, accepting her kiss of gratitude when he was done.

Then *she* was there. The woman who had swept into their world and turned it around, making him know what it felt like to have a beating heart again.

What it felt like to be utterly in love.

Tamara laid a hand on Sasha's shoulder for a moment before offering Caleb a quick hug and kiss. She stepped back and adjusted her new glasses. "Thanks for the present, but it's not my birthday."

"They look cute," he offered, dragging his fingertips down the tip of her nose as he admired the white frames decorated with small red roses.

"Oh, I have no problem adding another pair of glasses to my stash," she teased. "That's why I gave you my account information. Feel free to shop any time."

Sasha had the door open and was making motions for Emma to join her. "Come *on*, Emma. Who're you going to ride with? Mama or Papa?"

Emma looked torn, glancing between the two of them until Tamara laughed, picking her up and hugging her tight. "I don't know where we're going, but I'm pretty sure we have to ride there and then ride back. So why don't you ride with your Papa right now?"

His little girl gave Tamara a tight hug and kiss before she was lowered to the ground and hurried over to slip her hand into Caleb's.

He glanced around, suddenly floored by the fact he was

surrounded by so much love in the form of three different-size females. "Everyone ready to go?"

It came out grumblier than he'd meant, but they all hurried toward the horses, ignoring his mistake. In fact, Tamara came up under the pretense of making sure Emma was steady on the horse, slipping a hand around his neck before he mounted and pulling him to her for a kiss.

She looked him in the eye. "I love you," she whispered.

"I love you too." He couldn't get enough of saying it. He wasn't ever going to be done, and as he swung into position in the saddle and helped Emma hold the reins in front of them, he turned the horses toward their destination with a deep sense of purpose.

Some things were just meant to be.

TAMARA

They didn't seem to be going anywhere rapidly, but that was fine with Tamara. She sat on Stormy's back, swaying comfortably as their small group ambled forward at a relaxed pace. Sasha rode beside her, chatting endlessly about all the plans she had for the summer.

"And there's only ten more days of school, and after that we can help you with the garden more. And Daddy says that when I'm home from school for the summer, I can ride Firecracker every day."

"As long as you're with one of us, or one of your uncles, yes." It had been said before, but Tamara figured, with Sasha, it didn't hurt to repeat the reminder. "And you're not allowed to go into the arenas after the horses by yourself."

"Kelli can't take me? Kelli says riding horses is like freedom on four legs."

Tamara chuckled. "Kelli's very poetic for a ranch hand. But for now, no. You'll have plenty of chances to ride this summer with family supervising."

Sasha's pout couldn't last very long, not with the beautiful first-day-of-summer air and the sunshine heating the ground around them. Up ahead, Caleb was listening to Emma tell a story, the little girl speaking too faintly for Tamara to hear the individual words. But even that soft, steady murmur caused a little bit of a springtime-growing sensation in Tamara's heart.

Emma hadn't up and started speaking in full sentences overnight, but over the past months, she'd grown by leaps and bounds. Confident in the fact that she was loved. That she had people who chose to love her unconditionally.

Something inside Tamara's heart did another jiggly motion, almost like the Grinch's heart growing three sizes at once. Yes, she had pretty much fallen into a wonderful place. It wasn't what she'd expected nine months ago, but to go from losing her job to finding a family—

Life was pretty good.

It was clear by now where Caleb was leading them, turning off the trail onto the shortest route to Heart Falls. The trees closed around them, the rich scent of new growth turning the passage into a tunnel to Shangri-La.

They broke through the trees into sunshine. Ahead of them lay the sparkling pool at the base of the falls. The familiar rocks where she and Caleb had shared a fairly spectacular second meeting, and where she'd subsequently proposed to him, were to the right.

Caleb pulled to a stop and slid from his horse, ground-tethering her before reaching to lift Emma from the saddle. Tamara helped Sasha dismount, and the four of them wandered lazily along the edge of the pool, throwing rocks and skimming stones.

A soft, gentle moment of peace and quiet in the middle of what were hectic days for them all. The girls got busy, competing to see who could make their rocks *plunk* into the water with the biggest splash.

Tamara slid next to Caleb, leaning against him as he looped an arm around her waist. "Thanks for taking time out of your day to make this happen. It's nice to go for a ride with you in the sunshine."

Caleb pressed a kiss to her temple, squeezing her tight. "We'll do it more often." Then he pointed at the rocky lookout. "Go ahead. We'll meet you at the top."

"Bootstomp Point? Are you sure it's safe? You know big adventures always start there," she teased, dancing out of reach before he could smack his hand on her butt.

The girls caught the laughter, racing to catch up as Tamara led them onto the rocks to the peak where they had the best view of the pond. From that spot, when they glanced toward the waterfall, a perfect heart shape became clear.

Emma leaned against her, slipping her fingers into Tamara's. "It's like the heart gets love poured into it, and then it slips out at this end and runs all over Silver Stone."

Tamara smiled. That was not only a lot of words—it was a profound idea from the little girl. "There *is* a lot of love that runs all through Silver Stone."

Behind them Caleb cleared his throat. "Right. There's a lot of love in Silver Stone, but there's one thing missing."

Tamara turned to ask what he was talking about, momentarily distracted by the sight of someone walking the trail on the opposite side of the pond. A tall, dark-skinned gentleman paced his way around the edge of the pool, seemingly intent on joining them.

"What are we missing, Daddy?" Sasha asked. For some reason the words came out as if she'd practiced them a few times. Tamara glanced at her in confusion then back at Caleb, who was grinning widely.

"It's more of a technicality than anything else. Your mama

and I said that we loved each other, and that we're going to get married, and I've been thinking about it. We could do things up real fancy, but that's kind of not our way. So I wondered if you all would be okay if we just did the wedding thing, right here and now."

Married? Shock struck.

Not everyone, though. Emma made her opinion very clear as she let out a squeal of delight, bounced a couple of times, then stopped with a frown. "But I want to be a flower girl."

Caleb dipped his chin. "Thought of that."

He turned to greet the man who had made it to their side. The stranger was now recognizable as the father of some of Tamara's new friends in Heart Falls.

Malachi Fields offered a hand to Tamara and Caleb then passed a bag to Sasha. "Sorry I'm late. Are you ready to go?"

"Nearly." Caleb patted Sasha on the shoulder.

His oldest daughter grabbed Emma by the hand and scurried to a spot a little way off, dropping to her knees to dig in the bag for whatever Malachi had brought.

Tamara's brain was whirling. "We're getting married. Right *now*?"

Caleb pointed to Malachi. "Minister of the peace. And over there we have two flower girls who will be ready in about ten seconds."

Malachi grinned. Sasha and Emma had already bounced to their feet, flowery tiaras on their heads, and their hands full of something white and red.

While Caleb hadn't told her he planned this, they *had* talked about not doing anything fancy. His one sister was out of the country and wouldn't be back until late summer. His foster sister was having a big wedding in August. Tamara's sisters and the rest of the Coleman family couldn't get away from the ranch anytime soon, and it seemed rather than have part of the family there and not the rest—

Private and special was the way to go.

"We're getting married. Right now," Tamara repeated, no question in her voice this time as she watched happiness bloom in Caleb's eyes. "You're in charge. Tell me where I need to go."

"Over here, Mama."

Emma waved. Sasha held aloft a third flower circlet.

Tamara went willingly, dropping to one knee and leaning her head forward so her daughters—oh my word, her *daughters* —could arrange the red and white flowers.

Emma kissed her cheek and offered her a bouquet: daisies and teeny rosebuds.

"They match your glasses," Emma told her seriously.

Caleb had been tricky and artful. "I guess these are my wedding glasses," Tamara responded with a smile.

She stood to discover Sasha had crossed the distance to Caleb, slipping a rose into his front pocket. That's when it struck Tamara that his black shirt *was* a little fancy for going horseback riding, but then again, she wasn't past the thrilling part of staring at him no matter what he wore.

Malachi held up a finger then reached into his pocket and pulled out his phone. He pushed a few buttons, turned up the volume, and suddenly the familiar sound of a wedding march rang across the rocky expanse.

Tamara laughed, patting Emma on the shoulder. "Okay, flower girl. Have fun."

Emma reached into the bag, and the next second, a handful of rose petals flew through the air to lie scattered on the rocks underfoot.

It was one of those absolutely perfect moments that Tamara couldn't have dreamed up if she'd had a million years. Her cheeks hurt from smiling as she stood and lifted the bouquet in front of her.

She stared into the eyes of the man she loved as music played and the waterfall echoed—or at least she stared at Caleb between downward glances to make sure she didn't trip over the cracks in the rock.

Every time she looked back up, he was smiling harder, until the moment she put her hand in his and they turned together toward Malachi, who stood with his back toward the falls.

Sasha caught hold of Tamara's left hand, and Emma squirmed into the small space between Tamara and Caleb, and now the only music was the sound of the falls as Malachi led them through the ceremony.

Finally, Malachi asked them to face each other. "This part is up to you," he said. "You can't really do it wrong."

Unreal. Wedding vows beside a waterfall.

The girls stepped back all of two inches. Tamara offered her bouquet for Sasha to hold, then Caleb took both her hands, and his gaze turned fully to her face. His eyes were dark and serious, but she also saw the humour and joy in them that had become stronger over the past months as they fell more in love.

"Tamara Coleman, I take you to be my wife, my love, and my heart. Today, and every day, I promise to give you everything in me—body, spirit, and soul—and together we'll face the future. We'll laugh together and cry together and make a life together."

He slipped a ring onto her finger. She didn't even look down. All she wanted was right there before her, written on his face. Her stern, stubborn cowboy who was willing to give everything for his family, and she was so glad she got to be part of his world.

And now, it was her turn.

"Caleb—" Her throat tightened.

Oh my word, this was going to be harder than she'd imagined.

Sasha tugged on her hand, and Tamara glanced down to see Caleb's oldest holding her palm up, a ring resting on it. "It's for Daddy," she said firmly. "Don't drop it."

Laughter bloomed, and suddenly Tamara was able to speak, at least for a few moments. She bent and kissed Sasha's cheek as she took the ring. "Thank you, sweetie."

Tamara stood and faced the man she loved. "Caleb Stone, I take you to be my husband, my love, and my heart. I promise you're going to get all of me too, but because you sprung this on me, I don't have anything memorized that's as sweet as what you told me, but it's forever and sincere"—she turned her attention to Sasha and Emma—"and it includes you two. I take you to be my daughters. I'll be the best mom to you I possibly can."

With a soft cry of happiness, two little girls pressed against her as she turned back to Caleb. He had tears in his eyes as well, ones that hadn't been there until she'd included Sasha and Emma.

She knew where his heart lay. Firmly in *all* their hands.

She slipped the ring on his finger, but forget about getting a kiss—Tamara and Caleb stooped in unison to hug their two little girls.

It took a while until all the happy tears had been wiped dry, and they turned to Malachi, who was putting a handkerchief back in *his* pocket, smiling sheepishly.

"To not drag this out any further than necessary, I now pronounce you"—he held up one finger—"husband and wife" —a second finger—"and a family. May you love long and happily."

Caleb caught Tamara and, with their girls clinging tight, pressed his lips to hers, and they kissed for the first time in their married life.

It was a good day.

IF YOU'D LIKE to read Caleb and Tamara's story you can find it in **A Rancher's Heart,** the first book in The Stones of Heart Falls series.

PART II

—————

HEARTFELT AT HEART FALLS

Walker Stone and Ivy Fields are getting married, and all their family—even the goats—seem to want to be involved. Which is why Walker takes charge with a surprise to make this day perfect for both him and Ivy.

Timeline:

This vignette begins on the final day of **A Rancher's Bride** and the day before **The Cowgirl's Forever Love** begins.

IVY

March 1ˢᵗ, Silver Stone ranch.

Ivy Fields cautiously poked her head around the corner before stepping toward the horse stalls. "Walker?"

No answer.

Nothing but the usual sounds of the barn, which meant it was far from silent. Horses shuffled and nickered, buckets clanged, and a low rumble of voices carried from somewhere in the distance as the Silver Stone hands went about their day. Right where she was, though, were empty pathways and muted noises.

The sweet scent of clean hay tickled Ivy's nose, and she had to work to keep from sneezing.

Sneezing was to be avoided at all costs.

"Walker?"

She checked her phone again, but only the original message was there. He'd told her to meet him in the barn, but now that she'd arrived, he was nowhere to be seen.

Ivy sent off a quick message: *Where are you?*

Then she settled on a chair tucked to the side of the stalls, breathing deeply to allow the peacefulness of the location to wash over her. A moment of quiet in the bustle of everything that needed to be accomplished this Saturday wasn't a bad thing, although there were things that *needed* to be done because they had a deadline.

Tomorrow was their wedding day. Hers and Walker's. After so many years apart, they were finally back together and would be forever.

She closed her eyes as her lips curled into a smile. Life lately had been richly wonderful because Walker was—

Well, honestly, he was her heart.

Something nudged her thigh. She opened her eyes, ready to smile up at Walker.

A grey and white goat lifted its head in line with hers and blinked seriously.

Drat. One of the three pet goats belonging to Walker's nieces had escaped.

Again.

Ivy laid a hand on the creature's neck to keep it from moving any closer. Her fingers tangled on the bright-red bowtie attached to the animal's collar, and his name tag flashed, identifying which of them was currently annoying her.

"Okay, that's far enough, Meany."

He didn't agree, pushing harder, as if he wanted to give her a hug. Only she was *not* a goat hugger.

Ivy rose to her feet to brace herself better.

"Stop," she ordered in her best vice-principal voice, but Meany seemed determined to get up close and personal.

Ivy retreated, and the next thing she knew, she was pushed against the wall beside the tack room.

It seemed a little silly, but she didn't want to take on more than she could handle. While Meany wasn't that big, Ivy was a teacher, not a cowgirl. She knew from watching Sasha and Emma take care of their pets that if a goat wanted to, he could put up a fight.

Goat wrestling the day before her wedding was not on Ivy's agenda, so she quickly slipped into the tack room, partially closing the door to keep Meany out.

"Sorry, but you and I are not besties. You'll just have to find someone else to cuddle." She saw it in Meany's eyes. The utter sadness at being rejected.

Or maybe it was something far more evil, because he dipped his head slightly, narrowed his eyes...

Right before he turned around and kicked.

Ivy automatically jerked away. The motion hadn't been aimed at her but at something beside the door. A clatter rang out, then a crash, and the door jolted under her fingers.

Through the slight crack between the door and the frame, Meany grinned at her before turning on his heels. He stepped daintily for a couple paces then leapt easily onto the top of the nearest stall, doing an impossible balancing act. Another jump and he was strutting toward the open doorway leading outside to the arena.

"Brat," Ivy muttered as she went to open the door.

Nothing happened.

She pushed again even as she peered through the crack to try and see—

A large wooden box lay on the ground in front of the door, another just beyond it. They were wedged together tightly enough, that no matter how hard she pushed, Ivy couldn't make the door budge.

She tried for a solid ten minutes, though, because asking to be rescued would mean having to explain how she got into this situation in the first place.

It was no use.

"Good grief." Ivy laid her forehead against the solid wood panel and laughed. Beaten by a goat. Not one of her finer moments, but it was funny enough that she was able to appreciate the situation for the novelty factor.

Finally admitting defeat, she pulled out her phone and put through a call to Walker.

Less than five minutes later, the opening at the door widened to reveal his familiar, well-loved features. Curiosity shone in Walker's eyes, but there was also concern. "Interesting place to meet. You planning on a career change, Princess?"

She stepped into his arms, wrapping her fingers around his broad shoulders. Soaking in his warmth and letting the happiness in her tone assure him that she really was okay. "Meany was the evil mastermind of this tryst."

"Ah, yes. The goats of doom." Walker tucked his fingers under her chin and examined her closely before nodding, as if content to find she wasn't hiding anything. "I got waylaid by my brothers for a state-of-the-union update, and we were just finishing up when Meany dropped in. And then you called."

She would have explained more, but Walker slid a big hand around her neck and, with gentle but insistent strength, pulled her to him. Their mouths brushed fleetingly, then again. His lips soft against hers, teasing out the teeny bit of frustration that had risen at her predicament.

The kisses grew more heated as they continued. Walker laid his free hand against her lower back and brought their bodies into full contact. His hardness contrasted with her softness in such a perfect way, his lean lines and rock-solid passion making Ivy forget she'd been trapped by a goat. Forget that she still needed to finish getting ready for her wedding.

Forget the tomorrow she was both eager for *and* dreading, because celebrations meant a gathering, and even though they were *her* people, Ivy still never knew how she was going to react to a crowd.

Passion flared between her and Walker, intense and wild, the way it always did. White lightning and fire, they were ready to come together, so when he pulled them apart, it was far sooner than she expected.

He leaned his forehead against hers, breathing heavily as he used ironclad control to slow them down. "As much as I want to continue, we need to go help with the goats."

"Are we making a stew?" Ivy asked. "I could get on board with that—*oh!*" She ducked away, his fingers sliding off her butt. "*Walker*. No pinching."

"No suggesting cannibalism," he teased. "Those goats are family."

"Distant family," she insisted. "And they may not call me Auntie Ivy."

He laughed as he wrapped his fingers around hers and led her from the barn. "I like your coat, Snow."

She'd pulled on the bright-blue garment this afternoon because she knew it made him smile. "I love *you*."

He left her at the side of the goat pen with a fiery kiss then joined the chase for the elusive pets.

The four brothers worked with Sasha and Emma, although there seemed to be more arm-waving and excited shouting than goat-capturing.

A heavily pregnant Tamara was being escorted by her sister Lisa across the snow toward Ivy.

Ivy took Tamara's hand and helped her grab the railing for support. "Good to see you up and about."

Tamara grinned. "How could I miss even a single one of the wild goat escapades?"

Her sister looked puzzled. "I wonder if the girls are jury-rigging the pen to help the creatures get out because of how much excitement it causes."

The three of them paused, eyeing each other as they considered it, because really, it was possible.

Then Ivy had to shake her head. "Nope. I think it's one hundred percent evil goat power."

"Agreed. And for pity's sake, don't even *think* that idea again, Lisa, because if they could, my daughters would," Tamara warned sternly.

"Oh, no worries." Lisa glanced at the chaos, a smile on her face. "Nearly ready for tomorrow on our end," she told Ivy.

"Nearly ready on mine," Ivy offered brightly.

Lisa's head swiveled, and she gave Ivy one of those *looks*. The ones that said the woman knew Ivy was lying her pants off.

The next moment she found herself wrapped up tight in an enormous hug, Lisa whispering in her ear, "You're going to have an amazing day. I know you will. Trust me."

The sheer confidence in the message was enough to make Ivy's nerves relax a little. "Thanks," she whispered before joining Tamara at the fence.

Lisa backed away. "If you're both okay, I'll go help with the roundup."

Tamara waved her off.

So much to look forward to, so much happiness. Ivy considered how blessed she was as she and Tamara watched seven humans futilely chase three goats with boundless energy.

A lone rider appeared. A rope sailed out, but instead of falling over a goat head, it wrapped around Luke's shoulders.

His fiancée, Kelli James, moved closer to free him. Ivy deliberately turned so it didn't look as if she were watching, but it was impossible to look away as the two of them stole off together. Love was written on their every move.

Beside her, Tamara was laughing joyfully at her children and husband. The usually staid-and-stern Caleb appeared to be hamming it up with his children, and Ivy smiled at the sound of little-girl laughter.

When she glanced around to find Walker staring at her with love in his eyes, she nearly melted.

Whatever the next day brought, she'd be able to face it because Walker would be with her. Her heart, her rock-solid base.

Her love.

Walker winked then blew her a kiss.

The next moment, one of the goats ducked past Dustin's outstretched arms and rammed into the back of Walker's knees, and he cartwheeled to the ground.

WALKER

It just wasn't right. A day later and Dustin was *still* grinning every time he glanced at Walker.

"I will hurt you," Walker said as he passed his younger brother. They were in the Silver Stone ranch house kitchen getting ready for the wedding. "Stop now, or you will be sorry."

No one else had said a word about Walker's tumble. Of course, Caleb had been busy making goo-goo eyes at Tamara, and Luke had vanished with Kelli, but still...

It just wasn't right that his little brother had seen him taken out by a *goat*.

Dustin held his hands in the air. "Fine. It's your wedding day, so I'll be nice."

"Which means tomorrow you'll go right back to teasing, yes?"

His kid brother grinned again.

"Ass." Walker muttered it quietly in deference to the little people running around the room.

Dustin waggled his brows then headed off to answer a call for help from Tamara.

The next second, Lisa stood next to Walker. "Tansy called. They're on their way. Should be here in ten minutes."

Walker hadn't expected butterflies to strike, but they were there, taking control of his gut like when he used to lower himself onto the back of a bull.

"Oh, hey." Lisa patted her pocket and pulled out a folded piece of paper. "Your sister sent a letter a few days ago and said to give it to you now."

"Thanks."

He'd gotten an email from his foster sister Dare that morning as well, with well wishes from her and her husband, Jesse, and a promise to come visit soon.

He unfolded the page to find Ginny's familiar handwriting.

WALKER

You just don't take orders well, do you? I told you to wait until I'm back, but nooooo, you had to get married while I'm still off toiling in Italy.

Fine. I get it. I saw the way you looked at Ivy when I was there this summer. Go right ahead and start enjoying married twue luv a.s.a.p.

You two deserve it.

I mean that. You're an awesome big brother, and Ivy is wonderful, and I look forward to watching your wedding and crying.

(Trust me, that's a good thing. Chicks love to cry at weddings.)

Love ya, bro.

Your favorite sister named Ginny.

WALKER BLINKED HARD EVEN as he grinned. She was just so...*Ginny.*

He turned to Lisa, who was waiting patiently. "Thanks. You have everything set up?"

The idea had started so they could save the moment to share with his sisters, but then the truth had hit—Ginny and Dare weren't the only ones who would appreciate watching the wedding.

The rest of the agenda had grown from there.

Lisa pointed across the room to the television monitor brought up from the family room in the basement. A glorious image of an ice-clad waterfall graced the screen. Motionless, until you looked closer. Then it was possible to see delicate branches waving gently as the March wind moved whisper-like through distant treetops.

"I've got the recorder going," Lisa assured him. "I'm recording you guys *and* I've got a camera in the room here. It means you've got the legal witnesses you need, plus you'll get to see all of our reactions. So behave. Or not, your choice."

"Got it." Walker watched as his oldest brother stepped closer. "I think this is my cue."

Walker was caught up in a quick embrace as Lisa squeezed him tight. She let go then winked. "Happy wedding."

Caleb's hand came down on his shoulder before he could respond. The next thing Walker knew, he was outside, standing next to Hannibal, his horse.

Luke and Caleb joined him, arms folded over their chests. Expressions tight.

God. Just what he didn't need right now was bad news. "You're scaring me," Walker growled. "What's wrong?"

Caleb's face didn't change, but a muscle on Luke's cheek twitched a second before he gave up the act and broke into a wide grin. "Damn, knew I couldn't do it."

Their oldest brother rolled his eyes and shoved at Luke's shoulder. "Softie."

"Yeah, so sue me." Luke hauled Walker into a hug, patting him on the back hard enough to shake his teeth. "So happy for you, bro."

"Me too," Caleb agreed before pummeling Walker with equal enthusiasm.

"Hey, gentle with the bridegroom. If you break me, Ivy will give you both hell," Walker warned.

But this moment with Luke and Caleb was right and good. An affirmation of belonging shared with Walker's closest friends, who just happened to be his family. Just like the teasing with Dustin a few minutes earlier was right, and the note from Ginny—

Walker wouldn't have wanted it any other way.

And then she was there, and Ivy was all he could see.

She slipped from the car and he was there to take her hand, staring down at her in astonishment. "God, you're beautiful."

Her cheeks flushed, but she met his gaze straight on. "Thank you."

Ivy's mom and sisters gathered around to give final hugs before slipping into the house.

Her mom lingered for a moment. She cupped Ivy's face in her hands and stared with eyes full of love. "You *are* beautiful, sweetie, from the inside out. Because of who you are and how much you love. We're so proud of you, your father and I. Blessings to you on this special day."

Ivy's eyes were filling with moisture. "Mom..."

"I know, don't make you cry." Sophie Fields turned to Walker and shocked the hell of out him when she cupped his face. "And *you*. Your mom and dad would be so proud of the man you've become."

Walker's throat closed, and he was rendered speechless.

Sophie leaned in and spoke softly. "I know, don't make you

cry, either, but it had to be said." She kissed him on the cheek then stepped away. "Have fun, kids."

The house door closed, and suddenly it was just them. Him and Ivy standing on the snowy ground next to his horse.

Ivy examined him carefully, uncertain at this unexpected turn of events. "Umm, mind explaining what's happening?"

"Nope." He lifted her into his arms. Ivy let out a little squeal as she clutched his neck.

A moment later he was sitting in the saddle, Ivy firmly positioned sideways across his lap. Walker clicked at Hannibal and turned toward the mountains.

Ivy pressed her palm to Walker's face as she chuckled softly. "Is that a nope, you're not explaining, or a nope, you don't mind explaining?"

"It's a 'we're getting married, and neither of us really needs an audience' kind of thing." They were headed in the right direction at a nice, easy pace, so Walker focused on his bride. "I love you, Snow Princess. So damn much, I could stand on top of the tallest mountain and shout it to the heavens. But I don't need to have a bunch of people cheering us on—wait, that's wrong. We *do* need a bunch of people cheering us on, and supporting us, and for us to know that they're there for us. We've got that. Your family, and mine."

"Yet we seem to be headed away from the house where I'm pretty sure most of our family is gathered." Ivy's eyes softened. "And I'm wearing a puffy winter coat over my wedding dress."

Walker ran a hand down her arm as he admired her bright-blue coat and the bits of wedding dress he could see. There were little blue flowers with shining silver centers woven into her silvery-white hair, and she looked every inch the snow princess he'd fallen in love with all those years ago.

"God, you're so beautiful," he repeated, because he couldn't stop himself.

Ivy laughed as she hugged him tightly. "I love you, Walker Stone." She leaned away just far enough to look him in the eyes. "Does your secret have something to do with why my mother insisted I wear long underwear under my dress? Which I have to tell you was one of the most awkward conversations I've had with her in recent memory. Or maybe explain why my father left the house an hour before we did?"

Walker considered. "Probably?"

He told her where they were going and that the wedding would be recorded, then he proceeded to distract her for the rest of the ride by taking her down memory lane with a whole bunch of "do you remember...?" until they were both starry-eyed and laughing.

When they finally came to a stop beside the frozen pool at the base of Heart Falls, Ivy's cheeks were bright, and her eyes were shining.

Her father, Malachi Fields—who had been waiting patiently near the base of the falls—came forward to hold Hannibal's lead. Walker slipped off then lowered Ivy carefully to the ground. He left his hat hanging on the saddle, dragged a hand through his hair, and hoped like hell he didn't look too wild.

Malachi nodded at them. "Well, it seems it's time for the main event. Are you ready, Ivy?"

"Yes, Papa," Ivy whispered. "So ready."

He grinned and led them a few paces to the side, lining them up just right for the camera before taking a deep breath. "It's been my privilege to officiate at a few of these celebrations, but I'll admit that while every one of them was special, this one might just knock me a trifle off-kilter. So if I seem to become incapacitated, you two just go ahead and finish up without me."

Walker laughed then realized Malachi wasn't joking. "Yes, sir."

Ivy turned to face Walker, putting her hands into his, and he slipped into a bit of a dream world.

He knew the falls were there—a frozen magnificence of crags and nooks and shimmering meters-long icicles like only a wild winter wonderland could produce.

The sky overhead was a rich blue, and the air crisp on his throat with every breath, even though March had arrived like a lamb, and the temperatures were warmer than usual, a Chinook wind blowing.

Looking into Ivy's eyes made his breathing speed up. Made him focus down on the softness of her hands in his. On her long white skirt covered with teeny blue flowers that sparkled in the sunlight.

She was still wearing her puffy coat.

Malachi was talking, but Walker was fully focused on the woman he loved. On her face, and her lips, and the curve of her cheek, and the sweet memories he had of her here at the falls, and in his bed, and in his life, and everywhere.

He was so focused that when she grinned at him, he wasn't sure why.

He glanced at Ivy's father. "Did I miss something?"

"Son," Malachi leaned back slightly, his expression one hundred percent content. "The way you're looking at my daughter means you didn't miss a single important thing. Although if you'd like to tell her something about being together forever, this would be a good moment."

"Yes, sir." Shit. He was missing in action during his own wedding. Walker dragged a hand through his hair. Took a breath then started.

"Ivy, I thought about this moment and what I wanted to tell you, but it's pretty simple when it comes down to it. You know how I feel. I know how you feel. So if we keep working on it for the next fifty or more years, eventually we'll get it perfect. I'm looking forward to every minute."

He stopped, not sure what else to tell her.

That hadn't been romantic or sweet or any of those things. Poetry and roses he could only do in songs, it appeared, and he'd already done that for her.

Ivy's lips curled upward. "How *do* you feel, Walker Stone? How does loving me make you feel?"

Suddenly he was back on solid ground. "That one's easy."

He wrapped an arm around her, twisting until they faced the falls. He pointed at the very top, at the ledge he'd climbed to once. "Imagine yourself standing up there and then racing forward and throwing yourself off."

Ivy literally quivered in his grasp. "*Ummm....*"

He turned her so he could lean in, now eye to eye with her. "Loving you is a million times more thrilling and heart-pounding, and *god*, I'm never going to get enough of you. I love you, Ivy Fields, and I'm so grateful you're willing to be my wife."

She melted against him. "You're amazing. And while I don't think I could ever throw myself off the cliff, I'm ready to throw myself into forever with you. Thank you for loving me. Thank you for never stopping. I love you so much."

Screw protocol. When his woman said *I love you* as heartfelt as that, Walker needed to kiss her.

So he did.

He scooped Ivy up and, right there in front of a grinning Malachi, proceeded to kiss his bride before he'd been told he could.

The sun beat down on them, a flash of bright light bouncing off the surface of the pond and shining like a spotlight as Ivy returned his kiss.

Walker kept the exchange somewhat appropriate for public

viewing, separating them just enough to grin unashamedly at his new father-in-law. "So. Does this mean we're married?"

Laughter roared. Malachi nodded as his amusement shone clear and bright. "Sure. Why not? Welcome to married life, Walker and Ivy Stone."

A loud crack rang out, like a shot from a gun. The sound echoed as roaring filled the air. Behind them, the frozen surface of the waterfall reacted to the heat of the day, and a huge portion broke free from the top to fall with a deafening crash to the ground.

A chain reaction began, and as the air filled with a crescendo of bell-like clangs and shrieks and crackles, Ivy leaned against Walker's side. Together they stared in amazement as the entire wall of ice descended to the earth. Shattering shards flew everywhere, and with the sunlight reflecting off the ice, it was like a light show in the middle of the day.

It took a long time for the area to go quiet. Walker's heart was racing.

Ivy was breathing hard as she turned back to him. She shook her head slightly. "Walker Stone, this is the best wedding I could ever imagine."

He curled his hand around hers and squeezed tight. "Me too. Ivy *Stone.*"

Sheer delight shone in her eyes before Walker gave in to temptation and kissed her again.

Of course, that's when he remembered that all of this was being recorded. Everything from his loss of concentration to the ice fall and all the rest. He could imagine the laughter and cheering that would be happening at Silver Stone...

The memories being made and shared in a way that was perfect for both of them.

Walker let Ivy free but kept hold of her hand. "Want to wave at the camera with me?" he whispered.

Ivy blinked hard before nodding. "I forgot."

Good to know he wasn't the only one. "We were thinking about other things."

He twisted toward the camera, and they both waved.

Suddenly Walker found himself being pulled into a loving embrace as Ivy offered him another scorching hot kiss.

Laughter bubbled inside, and he caught her up in his arms and twirled her. Skirt flying, her long hair streaming behind them.

Love in her eyes as she stared into his.

"I love you," she repeated softly, just for him. "Now and forever."

The tumbleweeds had come home.

IF YOU'D LIKE to read Walker and Ivy's story you can find it in **A Rancher's Song**, the second book in The Stones of Heart Falls series.

PART III

—————

A WILD HORSE WEDDING

It's late April, and Kelli James is about to stir up some trouble for her fiancé, Luke Stone. Good thing there's nothing he likes better than her kind of mischief.

Timeline: This story takes place in the spring, about a month before **The Cowgirl's Secret Love** begins.

KELLI

Kelli James lay stretched out in the hayloft, straw poking into her backside as she stared at the dust motes drifting through the sunbeam above her.

It was pretty much one of her favourite places to be. The barn, where even now the horses shifted lazily in their stalls. The scent on the air was clean country, which meant not a lot of manure but tons of that rich, dirt aroma that lingered wherever animals lived.

Yep. It was her most relaxing getaway spot, yet she still felt her insides jittering worse than any time she'd been about to take on an animal with more energy than brains.

Floorboards creaked, but the faint whistle that accompanied the noise meant she didn't bother moving other than to let one arm fall across her forehead.

There was no time to hide the evidence beside her.

Luke's familiar chuckle tickled her ears. "You're looking very 'forlorn damsel in distress' with that pose. You been taking acting lessons from Lisa and Josiah?"

Kelli rolled onto her side as he settled on the hay bale to her right. No matter how frustrated she was, getting the chance to look over her man wasn't an opportunity to be missed.

One dark lock of hair had fallen across his forehead, the five o'clock shadow on his cheeks and jaw showing it was nearly the end of the day. Whatever he'd been working on, he'd gotten hot enough to roll up his shirtsleeves, which gave her a glimpse of his powerful forearms.

Muscles pressed against the fabric over his biceps, his jean-clad thighs only a foot away from her—

"You're looking pretty delicious," she said, ignoring his question. "What do you think our chances are of getting caught if I decide to jump your bones right now?"

He leaned forward, elbows resting on his knees as he stared down. "Pretty much one hundred percent. Although I have no objections to the bone-jumping on principle."

She curled up a little farther, sliding her hands along his thighs and moving in close so she could tilt her head back for a kiss.

The next moment, his arms were around her, lifting as he leaned back to drape her body over his. All the while the kiss went on. A little harder, a little more demanding.

The firm caress of his hands along her back and down to her butt set her motor flaring even hotter. His muscular body was rock-solid in all sorts of interesting ways.

A cough sounded from near the top of the stairs.

Luke's lips curled into a smile against hers. "Hundred and ten percent."

"It's a good thing I know you two so well." Caleb's complaint held a touch of amusement. Then he raised his voice, calling behind him. "Okay, girls. You can come up now. Auntie Kelli's here. She can help us find the kittens."

Her two favourite little people were about to arrive, so she pressed a final quick kiss to Luke's lips before murmuring a quick promise. "Jumping will happen later."

He patted her on the butt as he pretended to help her find her feet.

Kelli stifled a giggle as she greeted Sasha and Emma. "Is it kitten cuddle time?"

"Kelli says it's always kitten cuddle time." Sasha blinked. "I mean, *you* say that."

Emma nodded her head enthusiastically, sliding her hand into Kelli's.

God, these kids were cute. Although the fact that Sasha repeated everything Kelli said had become a constant reminder to watch her p's and q's.

"Well, I certainly don't want to interrupt kitten hunting." Luke's attempt to step aside was immediately squashed by Sasha grabbing him by the hand.

"You can stay, Uncle Luke. Kelli says cuddling kittens helps make people less cranky." Sasha stared up at him, head tilted to the side.

"Is Uncle Luke cranky?" Emma joined in the perusal before a little furl formed between her brows. "It's okay, I'll let you cuddle with my favourite kitten. It'll make you feel all better."

Oh my God. Out of the mouths of babes. Kelli glanced up at Luke, trying to hide her grin. "Well, we can't have a cranky Uncle Luke wandering around Silver Stone ranch, can we?"

Luke took it in stride, although he did glance over at his brother and give a warning frown. "No comments from the peanut gallery."

"I didn't say a word," Caleb insisted, raising his hands in protest. Then he rubbed his palms together and moved forward as if eager to get started. "Okay, girls. Let's go find some kittens."

They took off, crawling carefully across the hay bales, but not before Luke spotted the pile of magazines Kelli had been thumbing through. The ones all about creating the perfect wedding day and the latest fashions in wedding dresses.

The magazines that had been driving Kelli absolutely frantic ever since her girlfriends had presented her with the stack of them during a recent girls' night out.

Tracking down kittens was exactly what she needed to calm the wild butterflies in her belly.

Being engaged to Luke? Hands down the most wonderful thing that ever happened in her life. It meant getting to be with the man she loved more than anything. It meant being a part of a wonderful family and having a home.

The whole wedding dress business? Not sending a thrill through her. More like nausea.

"Come, Auntie Kelli." Emma's sweet voice. She'd climbed to the top of a section and was looking down past her hands in awe. Kelli joined her, enough happiness rushing up to get rid of all of the grumbly, cranky feelings that had been marring her happiness.

A brand-new batch of kittens was curled around their mama, contentment radiating from the little pile of furry perfection.

Warmth covered her back as Luke joined them, wrapping himself around Kelli like a protective blanket as he stared down, breathing slowly. Nuzzling his cheek against hers. "They look pretty content, don't they?"

She was content. Just like these baby kittens, being entangled in Luke's protective warmth was all she needed.

It was the simple things. It had *always* been about the simple things.

Sometime in the next few days, she was going to make that clear.

LUKE

Luke Stone was head over heels in love and completely miserable.

Being called on the cranky business hadn't helped, either. The fact his ten-year-old niece had clued in to the rumble in his gut was a pretty clear sign he needed to figure out a way to fix this, and soon.

And while cuddling kittens with Kelli was a short-term solution, not even the promise of wild, heart-pounding sex once they reached the seclusion of their own home could knock away the lingering frustrations.

Which meant it was time to do something about it because putting off the discussion wasn't going to make it any easier.

Caleb and Luke waited outside the barn for Kelli to finish giving Emma and Sasha good-night hugs and kisses. His brother eyed him carefully. "Want to talk about it?"

"Dammit, is there something written on my forehead in Sharpie?" Luke asked.

His brother shrugged. "It's clear you've got something on your mind. And I know things are good between you and Kelli, so it's not that."

Luke considered. "Just trying to find a path to make the right people happy."

"Hmmm." A measured look. "Bit of advice. Find the path that makes you and Kelli happy first. Anybody who doesn't like that path isn't one of the right people."

It was wonderful advice, only tough when Luke wasn't sure he and Kelli were headed in the same direction on this particular issue.

Still, he dipped his chin then impulsively offered his brother a back-pounding hug. "Thanks."

Caleb offered him a modestly sized grin as Sasha and Emma caught their papa by the hand and began taking him back toward the house where their mama and baby brother waited. "Let me know if I can do anything to help," Caleb called over his shoulder before giving his girls his full attention.

Kelli's firm grip wrapped around his fingers. "I'm ready to do some jumping, if you're still interested."

He glanced down, pausing when he spotted the armful of magazines she had tucked against her chest. "Definitely interested, but want to go for a ride first?"

She all but threw the magazines on the table at the side of the hall, whirling toward the tack room as he followed on her heels.

Like a well-oiled machine, they were soon out on the trail, sitting comfortably in their saddles as the warm spring night surrounded them.

Kelli held out a granola bar. "Don't want you getting *hangry*," she teased.

Considering he was making them late for dinner, it wasn't a bad idea. They ate while they rode quietly, the horses instinctively making their way toward the Heart Falls pool. It was one of the special places on the ranch, and Luke couldn't get enough of it.

It was a place where tough conversations could be had and still feel a little magical.

They ended up holding hands, arms hanging between their horses as they swayed in an easy rhythm toward the water's edge. Spring runoff made the falls a little wilder right now, the pond bursting at the seams as, everywhere around them, birds sang and new green leaves fluttered on the trees.

Kelli slipped off her horse, dropping the reins and letting him wander off to nibble on the fresh green grass.

Luke took her by the fingers and led her up onto the rocks where the perfect heart shape of the pool was clearly visible.

She slid an arm around his waist, head resting on his chest. "It's so pretty here."

He stared down at her. Her long brown hair, her beautiful eyes—staring out at the wilderness but holding tight to him. She looked as if she belonged here.

She definitely belonged in his arms.

Luke really needed to get over his issue. But ever since they'd visited her grandfather's estate in Kentucky, he'd been worrying over it. Having their friends Jack and Diane pop in had been wonderful, but it also compounded the problem.

Kelli stepped around to face him, sliding her hands up his chest. "I love you."

"I love you too." With everything in him. With every fiber of his being, which was why he had to just man up and either admit his issue or shut up and pretend it wasn't there.

Kelli lifted her chin firmly. "I have something to tell you."

She looked so serious. For one brief second, he panicked. "Are you...*pregnant*?"

She blinked. Her jaw fell open. "Oh my God, *no*. I mean, not yet. I mean, did you *want* me to be?"

"No. I mean, if it happened, I'd be okay with it, but I thought we were going to wait a little while. So it's okay if you're not." Luke was rambling. Definitely rambling.

The tension drained out of her, and she gave a sigh of relief. "Okay. Good. I just wanted to say that I love you, and I want to get married, but no way in hell am I going through with a wedding. I hope that's okay with you."

It was his turn to blink. "*What*?"

Her hands slid down, and she grabbed hold of his belt as if clinging for support. "The girls gave me all those wedding magazines, and while they're pretty and all that, the idea of picking out a wedding dress to crawl into—number one, it's a real waste of money because I'd only wear it one time. I mean, hello, that's just silly."

Luke had never thought of that. "I guess if it's something you always wanted…"

Kelli shook her head vehemently. "Then when we visited Grandfather Timothy, he talked about hosting a wedding there. Diane got into it as well, and I've been having nightmares ever since. I mean, they'd probably expect me to walk down that grand staircase. I'd be in that damn wedding dress that I don't want in the first place, and I could just see myself tripping and falling."

Amusement was beginning to rise. Why had he doubted for even a single moment? "So, what you're saying is no wedding. But you *do* want to get married."

She dipped her chin firmly. Then tilted her head hesitantly. "Do you mind?"

He picked her up, holding her close so he could rub their noses together. "You know what's had me cranky for the last while? Thinking about a big, fancy wedding at your Grandfather Timothy's house. Having to wait at the bottom of that big, long staircase for you to come marching down to me when all I want is to have you by my side."

"Get out." Kelli's face lit up. "That is really sweet, by the way."

They grinned at each other for a while. Luke spun her in a circle and got her laughing before lowering her feet to the ground. "Okay, then. Let's get married."

"Sounds like a plan. How do we do this? You want to go—" Kelli paused as he pulled out his phone and put through a call. Curiosity lit her face as she waited for him to speak.

"Malachi? Luke Stone here. Are you busy tonight?"

It took a lot less time than expected. He had to promise to send their already completed paperwork to Malachi a.s.a.p., but Luke hung up the phone with all kinds of happiness bubbling inside.

Kelli was all but vibrating with excitement. "What did he say? And holy hell, are you *serious*?"

Luke caught her by the hand, leading her toward the trail around the outside of the pond. Walking side by side toward the base of the waterfall. "He said he can be here in fifteen minutes."

She tugged him to a stop. "That means there's not enough time to call everybody."

He met her gaze square on. "We'll have a party to celebrate, and all our family and friends can be there. But this is about what's right for us. This is about us getting married. Period."

"I'm good with it," she promised. "I just had to point out the fact that no one else would be here so that I have you on record as saying it's also your decision."

Laughter rose. He guided her around the edge of the lake to where the rumble of water came pouring down, crashing against the pool's surface. They had to go one at a time, but the trail behind the falls was clear, noise echoing around them until they stepped once more into the open.

They'd been out of sight along the shoreline for maybe ten minutes, but it had been long enough for changes to occur.

Malachi was visible at the top of the trail, the tall, dark-skinned man moving steadily toward them. Their horses had moved along the shoreline and were only about ten yards from where they currently stood.

But it was to the far side of the pool that Luke and Kelli's attention shot. In the distance was a group of unfamiliar horses, and Kelli caught Luke's hand excitedly. "Wildies."

He glanced at her. "Really? I didn't think they ranged this far south."

"I heard from some of the old-timers down at Connie's that a big stallion moved into the territory." She glanced at their horses, whistling sharply.

The wild horses startled, shifting a little uneasily, but when nothing happened except the well-trained animals heading obediently toward Luke and Kelli, the herd went back to grazing.

By the time Malachi joined them, Luke and Kelli had their horses firmly tied to a tree at the side of the pool, far enough from the herd they couldn't get any ideas about running off.

Malachi glanced at the wild horses and then back at Luke and Kelli, who were now standing side by side, arms around each other's waists. "Well, this seems rather appropriate. I take it you're on board with this idea as well, Ms. James?"

"Tell me when to say *I do*, because I do," Kelli assured him.

The older man ran a hand over his head, the silver grey at his temples contrasting with his black hair and dark skin. "Well, then, let's get to that part of the show. We'll worry about signatures, witnesses and paperwork after. That's the relatively unimportant part."

Holy cow. They were actually going to do this. Kelli's fingers slipped into Luke's—slightly cool, strong and yet soft.

Malachi cleared his throat. "We're just going to do this the really simple way. Luke, you have something you want to tell Kelli?"

Everything. He wanted to tell her everything, but the truth was they had forever ahead of them. He had a lot of tomorrows to continue to tell her again and again.

Luke turned her toward him, catching both hands in his. "You're perfect for me. You make me laugh, and you make me smile. You make me want—not just physically, but to be a better man. I love you, Kelli. And I'm going to make sure you know that every day. Because you're my heart."

Kelli was blinking back tears. "Dammit. This is another reason why I didn't want to have a wedding. Can you just imagine, standing in front of everybody with a snotty nose and running eyes in a fancy dress that doesn't even have pockets?"

A deep rumble of laughter shook Malachi.

Kelli reached into her jeans and pulled out a handkerchief, wiping her eyes dry and getting herself back together. The laughter Luke had mentioned was welling up inside. It was about to burst out, and there was no way he could contain it.

Then Kelli squared her shoulders, and before Malachi could prompt her, she began having her say.

"Luke Stone, I love you. I think I've always loved you. And I can't believe you mentioned sex in our wedding vows, but at the same time I *can* believe it, because all said and done, I really like that part of life with you. I also like that we talk all day and still have things we want to talk about at night. I like that we work together, and play together, and just enjoy life together. And I'm glad we're getting married, because I want to keep doing all of it with you, forever."

Impulsively, she threw herself into his arms, and he caught her, squeezing back tightly and barely catching his breath before their lips connected and she was kissing him fiercely.

"That's about as official as it needs to be," said Malachi, and amusement rumbled in his voice. "Mr. and Mrs. Stone."

Luke slowly stopped kissing Kelli but kept her in his arms.

She pulled back just far enough to offer her friends' father a mischievous grin. "No telling Tansy or Rose before I get a chance."

"I wouldn't dream of it," Malachi assured her. He glanced at Luke then back at her. "Congratulations. I wish you a lifetime filled with love and laughter, but considering who I'm talking to, that's pretty much a given."

Kelli wiggled her way to the ground, giving Malachi a huge hug before coming back to tuck herself into Luke's side. "Thank you."

"My pleasure."

At the far side of the pool, a loud whinny rang out. The wild stallion walked toward them, mane shaking as he made his presence known. He dipped his head momentarily then called out again before moving around his herd and guiding them back to the trees.

Malachi stared after the wild horses. "Just when I think I've seen it all. That's the first time I've ever had a herd of horses act as witness."

It was a perfect moment. A little on the wild side, filled with horses, just him and Kelli.

Luke waited until Malachi was marching back up the path before he scooped Kelli up in his arms, pacing forward eagerly.

Kelli held on tight even as she grinned at him. "Hello, *husband*. Where are you taking me?"

The roar of the waterfall picked up in volume as Luke made his way back along the trail. "I thought I'd have a little private celebration with my wife. Like that idea?"

She considered for a moment before nodding briskly. "I didn't get a chance to say it before, but it seems appropriate now. I do. Hell yes, I do."

So they did.

IF YOU'D LIKE to read Luke and Kelli's story you can find it in **A Rancher's Bride,** the third book in the Stones of Heart Falls series.

PART IV

OH BABY!

A cute puppy, a wedding, and a baby. that's it. That's the blurb.

Longer cheater version:

Lisa and Josiah are thoroughly enjoying each other's company. He's got his veterinarian work; she's been busy stepping in to help her sisters and friends whenever and wherever they need. And they have Ollie, the sweet little terrier that can't get enough of either of her favourite humans.

But as one year ends, and a new one begins, Lisa can't help but wonder if there's something she's missing. What exactly is she supposed to focus on now that her extended family is settled and all her sisters are happy?

Ollie knows...

Timeline: Action begins immediately after the conclusion of *The Cowgirl's Chosen Love.*

CHAPTER 1

New Year's Eve, Heart Falls

A shriek of laughter rang from the back deck. Lisa glanced up from where she was preparing hot boozy drinks to discover her youngest sister had both hands raised, pleading for mercy.

"I give up. I didn't mean it. I will never do it again—Zach. *No.*" Julia shouted again, louder this time, as her boyfriend—sort of husband/the guy she was living with—lifted her onto his shoulder and spun her in a circle.

"Sneak attacks are good and fine, but you're supposed to sneak up on the *other* team, Mischief," Zach told her even as amusement shook his words.

That's when Lisa noticed the remains of a snowball scattered across Zach's broad shoulders and tangled in his brown hair. He all but bounced his way to the side of the deck, chuckling evilly the entire way.

Julia screamed for real as he tossed her off the edge then dove after her, while puffs of snow shot skyward. Earlier that day Josiah had used the tractor to move some of the recent massive snowfall into a pile right up against the deck, creating a safe but frigid sliding spot for their New Year's Eve family gathering.

Lisa was so pleased to welcome all her sisters and their partners for the final celebratory gathering of the year. It promised to be a wonderful chance to catch up with everybody, including Julia and Zach, who had just returned from their holiday getaway in Hawaii.

Even as Lisa glanced around with deep satisfaction, she was self-aware enough to admit something wasn't right. Some problem was tickling at the back of her brain—

She'd worry about it tomorrow. Right now, there was too much family and chaos to enjoy.

Another snowball flew past her, smacking hard into the glass beside the back door.

Lisa's oldest sister, Karen, shouted with a laugh, "Dammit, Finn. Stop dodging. If I break a window, Lisa will have my head."

Finn Marlette stepped out from around the corner, his usually unreadable expression as close to a smirk as Lisa had ever seen. "Sure, *ma chérie*. Blame your target for moving."

The next instant he gasped as a multitude of snowballs pummeled his forehead and torso. They shattered, raining around him as if he were the center feature in a snow globe.

"I yield." He put his hands in the air. One final missile exploded against his chest, and he turned a mock glare toward Lisa. "Hey. I raised the white flag."

Lisa brushed the snow off her hands then reached for the tray of hot chocolates laced with peppermint schnapps that she'd prepared. "Strange. I could've sworn I threw that *before* you admitted defeat. There must be some sort of time-bending mischief happening, right here in my backyard."

"Strange, my ass." Karen snickered as she moved aside to let Lisa pass. "Good throw, sis."

"Why, thank you."

It took a while, but eventually they had all gathered around the fire pit. Four couples wrapped up tight in layers of clothing and blankets in spite of the flames flickering before them.

Lisa curled her fingers a little tighter around her mug, leaning against the strong, steady torso of her favourite person in the whole wide world. Without skipping a beat, Josiah Ryder slid an arm around her, cuddling her close even as he responded to the question Finn had just asked.

Tucked into the cushioned loveseat on her opposite side, the cream-coloured terrier who owned her and Josiah wiggled into a slightly more comfortable position. Ollie rested her chin on Lisa's leg so she could stare up at them both with her usual devotion.

Cozy. Comfortable. It was an evening full of family, and as conversation drifted easily amongst them, Lisa reflected on how much things had changed over the past year.

She had to admit that while they'd had their ups and downs, it had all been worth it.

A year ago, she'd been living at her sister's home, helping take care of her family while Tamara dealt with a difficult pregnancy. Now seated across from Lisa, Tamara's shiny yellow glasses glinted in the firelight as she laughed at something her husband, Caleb, said. The two of them held hands, the simple connection as big and solid as any neon lights, declaring they were together.

Karen and Finn sat to their right, and Julia and Zach to their left. All four of the Whiskey Creek women were gathered in what was definitely not Whiskey Creek.

It seemed safe to declare that Heart Falls was now their home.

Zach cleared his throat. "Not to interrupt the celebration, but—"

"—but you're going to do it anyway," Finn finished in his measured drawl. He waved a finger. "Don't ever say you don't like to be the center of attention."

"Can I help it that I'm so memorable and intriguing?" Zach pressed a hand to his chest. "Natural charm added to deliberate modesty equals one spectacular specimen."

Finn made a gagging sound. Beside him, Karen smacked him softly with her mitt, but she snickered as the banter continued for a bit longer.

Josiah leaned against Lisa's side, positioning his lips near her ear. "Those two are dangerous together."

"You're just happy somebody else is being a drama queen," she teased.

A snort escaped him, drawing attention from the rest of their crowd.

Josiah grinned innocently. "So, Zach. You were saying?"

The other man offered a wink. "Julia and I got back late last night from Hawaii."

"That would explain the tans," Tamara offered dryly. She twisted slightly, leaning forward to speak directly to Julia. "Could you poke him so he'll get to the point?"

"We got divorced." Julia blurted the words but held up a hand as confused questions began to rise. "It's okay, because we're going to get married. I mean married again, for real. Only this time not in Vegas and not fueled by tequila."

Lisa's mind spun through the statement, analyzing and coming to one very fine conclusion. Her sister's accidental marriage being on and then off was a good thing. "If that means what I think it means, congrats."

Zach grinned. "Thanks."

A round of well-wishing went around the loop, and everyone stood to exchange hugs and the rest of it.

They had just finished settling back into their chairs when

Zach caught Julia's fingers and pressed a kiss to her knuckles. "Also, she asked *me* to marry her." His grin outshone the fire as he looked around at the other guys, definitely gloating. "Just because you needed to know that."

Josiah coughed lightly and glanced at Finn.

Finn glanced at Caleb.

The sturdy cowboy with a heart of gold and a gruff exterior eased back in his lawn chair, fingers once again tangled with Tamara's. "Well. That's a fine thing."

"Isn't it just? I figure it's a pretty big sign that we've got something special here." Gloating. Yup, Zach was definitely gloating.

Caleb nodded. "Damn right. You know, when Tamara proposed to me, I figured that was one of the—"

"She proposed to you as well?" Zach looked almost disappointed for a moment before he perked up. "That's awesome."

"Karen offered to propose," Finn informed him. "Just in case you're keeping track."

"Well, damn. It seems as if the Whiskey Creek Colemans like to do things a little less traditionally." Zach was the first, but only seconds later, every set of eyes had turned toward Lisa and Josiah.

Oh, hell no.

Beside her, Ollie jerked to alert, probably sensing Lisa's increased tension. She ran a hand over the pup's head, soothing her to cut off the whine that had begun.

Lisa deliberately stared her way around the circle. "Josiah and I have discussed the marriage topic but came to the conclusion that our relationship does not need any institutionalizationism."

Karen snickered. "Please promise you'll finish two more of these drinks and then repeat that word. I want to hear you tie your tongue in knots."

It was too tempting to resist—Lisa stuck out said tongue at her oldest sister and soaked in the ensuing laughter.

They sat together for the next couple of hours, sharing stories. Offering up plans for the coming year.

"Business as usual for me at the Heart Falls veterinary clinic," Josiah offered. "Thank you for your continued support of my services."

"You offer a family rate. We appreciate it," Finn said sincerely.

"The family keeps growing. I'll have my hands full with Tyler, along with Sasha and Emma. It's Sasha's last year before becoming a teenager, if you can believe it." Tamara raised her brows at Caleb. "I hope you're ready for this."

"Of course we are. Besides, if she gets any ideas about straying off the right path, we'll sic Kelli on her." Caleb said it with an absolutely straight face. "If we tell her *Kelli said* she needs to clean up her act, it'll be as if God spoke."

Karen laughed. "Let's hope that continues to work. But your kids are great," she assured Caleb before turning to meet Finn's gaze. "We're going to get Red Boot ranch operational by the spring. Test run a few smaller groups then head into full operation by the middle of summer."

"If that's what the foreman says, then it's got to be true." Finn dipped his head. "She's a smart cookie, that one."

Karen beamed.

"I'm staying on as medical officer," Julia said proudly.

"I love getting to work with you," Karen returned, smiling at the woman who had only come into their lives during the past busy year. "Zach, did you decide if you're moving ahead with your brewery idea anytime soon?"

"Still researching," he admitted before offering a chin tilt in his best friend's direction. "Finn and I want to make sure Red Boot ranch is in the black before I take on too much else."

The group of them rang in the New Year, cheers rising skyward as the clock ticked past midnight. Everyone turned to their partner for a good-luck kiss, and as Josiah pulled her close, Lisa was definitely counting her blessings.

His lips against hers were warm and yet demanding. There was no getting distracted when he wanted her full attention. Except for—

An excited *yip* sounded by their ankles, and Josiah's mouth curled into a smile before he'd even finished the kiss.

Their foreheads touched briefly. "Somebody else wants to say happy New Year."

Lisa swooped down and grabbed Ollie, cuddling the pup between her and Josiah. "Yes, you need to be part of the celebration as well," she told the little terrier seriously. "Happy New Year, Ollie."

She pressed a kiss to the dog's head then lifted her gaze to meet Josiah's.

"Don't let your sisters see you do that," Josiah warned in a whisper.

"Too late," Julia whispered in return as she walked past, tugging Zach with her.

It wasn't much later that everyone left, headed back to their own homes. Tamara to a nine-month-old baby boy and the rest of her and Caleb's family she cared for as a full-time mom. Karen was off to the big ranch house she and Finn were renovating while getting the ranch up and running. Julia and Zach were the last to go, discussing ideas for building a place of their own as well as dealing with their tasks for Red Boot ranch.

Lisa and Josiah put away a few things before leaving the rest for the morning.

"What do you think about starting the new year right?" Josiah asked the question with a voice that had gone deep as he crowded her down the hallway toward their bedroom cautiously, to avoid kicking Ollie, who kept pacing underfoot.

"That's a wonderful idea," Lisa said with great enthusiasm. She wrapped her fingers around his collar and smiled up demurely. "It's very important to get at least eight hours of shut-eye, so we should probably hit the sack right now and go straight to sleep."

He slipped their bodies into alignment and let her know exactly what kind of activity he had in mind. "Tease."

"Never." Lisa said softly. "I love you. Last year, this year, and every moment into the future."

Ollie was sent to her bed in the corner with a firm directive to stay. The agenda after that faded into loving. The night had been as close to perfect as possible from beginning to end.

Only when Lisa woke, sun shining across the bed and turning the first day of the new year into something shiny and bright, the problem that had been itching the back of her brain revealed itself crystal clear.

Everyone in her family had goals set for the coming year. Everyone had a job to do. Everyone.

Except her.

CHAPTER 2

February 1ˢᵗ

Josiah hurried through the barn, headed back to the house, and Ollie danced at his heels. "You didn't tell Lisa the surprise, did you? Of course not. You know how to keep secrets. You're such a good girl."

He stopped before opening the door, kneeling and pulling out a dog treat for Ollie. He scratched behind her ears as she daintily gobbled it down.

The year was flying past. Between dealing with a few unfortunate time-consuming disasters at the veterinary clinic and the reality of keeping in touch with what was now a very large extended family, it was already the beginning of February.

Work had been outrageously busy. Josiah was so thankful he'd hired a new vet, Yvette, right before the holidays. Having a skilled set of hands who knew the clinic and had already met many of their clients had been vital for keeping things on track, especially since his long-time receptionist Sharon had needed time off the past couple of weeks.

Having Lisa in his world had been the sweet icing on the busy chaos. Waking up every morning with her made him feel as if he'd won the lottery. And since she'd been filling in for Sharon at the front desk, he'd gotten to see her and talk to her even more than usual each day.

The not-so-wonderful part was that something was wrong. He'd noticed it in particular during the last couple of days. Coming into the house to discover Lisa staring off into space, although she always pulled herself together quickly when she spotted him.

He wasn't worried that there was something wrong between *them*. Lisa Coleman loved him with every atom in her body, and he knew that to the tips of his toes now. She'd picked him for forever. On that score, he had zero doubts.

Only there were times while driving down the gravel roads, nothing but snowy fields surrounding them, that he wondered if she missed the idea of travelling to warmer places. Seeing things other than familiar ranch houses and miles of fence posts that ran all the way to the horizon.

He couldn't do anything right now about the fact they were stuck in snowy Heart Falls with no chance to go exploring for a bit, but he could do something to make staying home more exciting.

Luckily, she'd agreed to pick up a few groceries without even blinking, giving him a chance to get home and set up her surprise.

Josiah had it all planned out, but at the last moment, instead of heading up the spiral staircase to the loft room at the top of the silo, he decided to arrange things in their bedroom. It was a little closer to the shower in case things got messy.

He was such an ass that the thought of getting messy with her only made him grin that much harder.

By the time the front door opened and Ollie rushed toward

Lisa to offer a quick bark hello and as many kisses as she could slip in, Josiah was casually sitting in the recliner in the living room, pretending to poke through the latest *Veterinarian Report*.

Lisa caught his eye. "Hey. You beat me home."

"I did." He got to his feet and came to relieve her of the grocery bags in her hands. "Any more out there?"

"This is it. Are we having a cheese fondue tonight?" she asked eagerly. "Not that we have to, but I kind of noticed that you had a lot of the things that go into one on the list, just saying."

He stood there, grocery bags dangling from his hands as he leaned forward and pressed their lips together, answering her right before they connected. "We're doing all sorts of things tonight."

The kiss was sweet and perfect. The taste of her settled every bit of the worry he'd had. When they pulled back, he offered a wink. "Let me put these things away. You go and slip into something—"

At the front door, Ollie bounced up and down as she barked loudly and enthusiastically, peering out the side window into the yard.

"Ollie. Hush," Lisa scolded, stepping toward the door to see what was setting the dog off. "Holy *shit*."

Not good. Josiah dropped the grocery bags to the floor and came to press against Lisa's back, peering over her shoulder. "Who are you so disappointed to see?"

Standing on the front porch outside the door was most definitely not any of their friends or family. Instead, an enormous winged bird with a somewhat rectangular head and a triangular beak pecked on the glass at eye level.

"Is that an ostrich?" Lisa demanded.

"I think emu. Right now I'm more concerned with *how the hell* than *what the hell*," Josiah admitted.

"Is it dangerous?"

"They're mean and nasty, all right. It's probably in more danger from freezing, though." Josiah glanced down at their feet where Ollie was just about tripping him as she bounced her paws off the safety glass, still barking at a high volume and a furious rate.

"Ollie. Be quiet." Lisa went to scoop the terrier up in her arms, cursing softly as Ollie wiggled to get free and return to keep an eye on the front door. "Stop it, or I'll drop you."

"I'll shut her in the bathroom for now," Josiah suggested, taking the squirming dog from Lisa's arms. "She's trying to defend us from the alien invasion."

Lisa peeked out the window again. "Emus in Heart Falls. Wow."

"Why don't you put the groceries away then meet me back here, and we'll see what we can do about wrangling up our visitor."

It wasn't exactly the start to the evening that he'd been hoping for, especially with Ollie continuing to carry on as if the only thing keeping her favourite people alive was her franticly yipping over and over again.

In the end, he and Lisa pulled on their winter coats and headed outside, cautiously working to herd the emu into a safe corner of the barn. "Obviously somebody local has been keeping exotic pets."

Lisa stared into the pen where they'd put the tall creature. "Better than a cougar, I guess—my cousin in Rocky had to deal with that situation once. It was terrible."

"Wild animals as pets is one of my least favourite things," Josiah agreed. "Cougars are bad. The guy who had an entire pack of meercats, though, that was both messy and dangerous."

"Get out," she gasped.

He wrapped an arm around her and guided her back to the

house. "Let me make a quick post to get the information about our guest out on the local veterinarian loop. While I do that, how about you get into that something comfy I mentioned?"

She glanced up from under her lashes. "Why, Mr. Ryder. You seem to have something nefarious on your mind."

"Definitely. I put what I want you to wear on the bed."

Her pupils dilated as she pressed against him, walking her fingers up the placket of his shirt. "Is it pretty? Is it soft? What if I don't like it? Maybe I'll put on whatever I want."

Oh, really? Someone was feeling mischievous. Josiah wrapped a hand around the back of her neck. "Changed my mind. You're staying right here."

She hummed happily, sexual interest shining from her eyes.

He couldn't wait. He'd never had a problem with control before, but it seemed no matter how elaborate the plans he came up with, a seemingly innocent touch of her lips against his was all it took to make him lose it. He wanted to toss everything out the window except wrapping himself around her and connecting them on an intimate level.

He tangled his fingers in her hair, tightening them into a fist firm enough to tilt her head back for him to ravish her mouth. Although, was it ravishing when she was as eager as he was? Lisa nipped and bit, catching hold of the fabric of his shirt and jerking it free of his jeans.

Dammit. He had so many ideas, but ninety percent of them vanished as her taste drilled through him. Excited gasps and moans escaped her lips as he stripped away her T-shirt and put his teeth to her neck. Undoing her bra, cupping her breasts in his hands so he could lean down and suck the tips hard.

"*Yes,*" Lisa breathed out before whimpering. She clutched his shoulders, nails digging in. When she lifted one leg and hooked her knee around his hip, it lined them up perfectly, and he rocked his erection against her soft, sweet center. "That feels so good."

He'd put on music before she'd gotten home, and the tune changed to a heavy beat that pulsed in time with his heart. "Dammit, Lisa."

She knew exactly what he was complaining about, because this wasn't the first time one of their fun scenarios had gotten out of hand and gone faster than expected. "I want you now."

Josiah groaned. Her hands were between them, undoing his belt buckle, scrambling at the button of his jeans. He had no intention of stopping her. He still wanted to give to her. Everything, all of it. "*Lisa—*"

She turned in his arms, shoving at her own jeans. An instant later her naked ass pressed against him, trapping his erect cock against heated skin. "Fuck me."

Goddamn. The plans he'd made could wait. He slid his hand over her belly, fingers capturing her mound. Holding her. Controlling her as he tilted his hips until his cock slid between her thighs. "A little bit mouthy tonight. I like it. Only, you weren't very specific."

Her thighs were clamped tight around his cock, and working himself back and forth against her heated skin was enough to keep his body buzzing. It gave him time to slick his fingers through her folds and begin teasing at the entrance to her sex.

Over the past months, they'd experimented a whole lot, finding out what really made each other hot. Lisa could come hard and fast from him playing with her pussy if he did it right.

She shuddered, reaching a hand back to catch hold of his hip. "Josiah. I want your cock."

"This first." He slid his fingers into her sex, thumb resting over her clit. He moved slowly, teasing with tiny pulses. Rubbing his fingers against the sweet spot just inside her folds.

Lisa's head fell back on his shoulder, and her legs quivered. "Yes. Oh, *yesssss.*"

Heat wrapped around them. Josiah pressed his other hand between her breasts, their upper bodies tight. He still wore his shirt, the tails tangling between them. Both of them with their jeans around their ankles.

"Close," she warned.

A loud howling rang out from the bathroom. Ollie, complaining that she'd been so cruelly abandoned.

Josiah squeezed his eyes shut and concentrated, catching hold of Lisa's breast and tweaking her nipple in the hopes of giving her what she needed to take the final—

She moaned. Gasped. Said his name, the vowels quivering as her hips pulsated against his fingers. Before he was done helping her ride the aftershocks, she pivoted again, leaning back against the wall. Hands splayed on either side of her hips for balance, she stared at his rigid cock.

"Finish."

He was seconds away from doing exactly that. By the time he found a condom, this moment would be past, so he wrapped his fingers around his length and pumped. Meeting her eyes then letting his gaze trickle down over her breasts, which showed the marks of his hands. Of his five o'clock shadow.

"So sexy," Lisa said, teasing fingers across her own belly and returning to stroke her clit.

"Show me," Josiah demanded.

She pulled open her folds and let him see her clit peeking out from skin gone swollen and red from her orgasm, moisture glistening. Her long fingers were wet as she stroked herself.

"Fuck." He came, long spurts shooting across the distance between them. His come landed in white streaks on her belly, on the curls of her mound, and her fingers. His head spun, but as she dipped her fingers in and out again, he groaned her name. The final bits of pleasure stripped from his body.

Josiah damn near fell to his knees because he couldn't stand. He pressed his hands to her skin and teasingly rubbed the moisture all over her.

"Mine," he growled.

Lisa's belly shook under his fingers as she laughed. "That was awesome."

He glanced up, the love in her eyes shining so clearly. "Thank you for letting me ravish you in the front hallway. That wasn't the plan for the evening. Just so you know."

She tucked her fingers under his chin and met his gaze straight on. "That's good. That means we still have something else to look forward to tonight."

"I love you." Not saying the words would be like not breathing.

Her smile went impossibly bright. "I love you too."

Ollie howled a complaint.

"And *she* loves us, only she'd really like to be right here next to us to tell us in person," Josiah interpreted for Lisa.

"Well, naturally." Lisa stepped out of her jeans and panties, waiting until he'd done the same. She piled all her clothes into his arms. "Here. I'll go rescue Ollie. Once she's settled in her bed, I'll join you in the shower."

It was a fantastic idea.

It was a fantastic evening.

The next morning, Lisa was still smiling. Her fondue and the massage parlour he'd organized in their bedroom both having satisfied her immensely.

She topped up his coffee before resettling in the chair beside him. "Did you get any leads on our exotic visitor?"

"Nothing on the board yet, but it's early enough that not everybody would've checked. We'll do some more research once we hit the office on Monday if I don't hear anything sooner." He glanced at her. "You're still filling in for Sharon this week, yes?"

"She sent an email saying she's ready to get back to work *next* Monday. Which means yes, if you want to enjoy any office hijinks, Dr. Ryder, this week is your last chance." Lisa waggled her brows.

"It's been nice working with you," Josiah said honestly. "I know desk jobs aren't really your thing. Thanks for helping out."

Her nose wrinkled for a moment, even as she nodded. "No problem."

There it was. Everything from her tone of voice to the change in how she sat said there was a problem. He leaned in closer. "Lisa? Sweetheart, what's wrong?"

She blinked. "Nothing."

That also was very clearly the truth. Which meant Josiah was now thoroughly confused.

Ollie wandered over, resting her chin on his knee. He glanced down at the dog. "I am having a hard time getting a read on this patient," he said as if consulting with Ollie. "I have a feeling that maybe even she doesn't know what's wrong."

Lisa snorted, and he glanced up just in time to catch her finishing a massive eye roll. "Please. I'm not one of your barn animals for you to do your animal-whisperer thing to."

"It would be easier if you were," Josiah mock complained. "Babe, it seems as if there's something on your mind. Which isn't a bad thing, and I'm not demanding you talk if you're not ready, but when you are, *if* you are, I'm here."

Her head fell to the side, and she smiled at him with an entirely different expression. One of complete adoration.

It was an awful lot like the expression Ollie often wore, not that Josiah was going to tell Lisa that.

She nodded slowly as if thinking it through. "It's more of a weird revelation than something wrong."

Josiah leaned back in his chair and gestured for her to go on. "Revelations can be good."

"They can."

"And what have you discovered?" Josiah encouraged.

"In one week, I'll be unemployed," Lisa said. "And thinking about that reminded me that I basically haven't had a job in my entire life."

CHAPTER 3

The expression on Josiah's face made Lisa snicker.

He blinked, hard, as if trying to make sense of what she'd just thrown at him. "That's not true."

"It totally is," she insisted. "I'm not going to be silly about this. I'm not claiming that I've never *worked*. But the truth is, when I started thinking about everything that I've done over the years, all of it just kind of happened. I have never done a job interview. I have never applied for a job. I have never had a job *title*."

"You're a cowgirl," Josiah said instantly, which was really sweet, but not the point she was trying to make.

"I've driven a tractor, and I've plowed a field. I've also helped shoe a horse, inoculate piglets, and deliver way too many calves. How many of those things have you done?" She leaned back and folded her arms over her chest. "All of them, I'd bet. Because you're *Dr.* Ryder. Veterinarian, who applied for and went to school to get that title."

Josiah's gaze narrowed. "I'm listening, but I'm not catching the gist of what you're saying."

Lisa waved a hand in the air. "This is probably why I haven't brought it up. I'm not even quite sure *what* I'm complaining about. Or if it *is* a complaint." She struggled to verbalize what was going on inside. "You know when you get together with a group of people for the first time? Everybody goes around the circle and introduces themselves."

This time he gave a decisive nod.

She offered him a soft smile. "They say their names, and where they're from, and what they do."

"Oh." Josiah frowned. His expression folded into concern. "You don't have to fill in at the clinic if you don't want."

"Oh, this isn't about that at all," Lisa assured him. She abandoned her cup on the table, moving in closer until she could steal his coffee cup as well and then claim space in his lap. She squeezed him tightly, holding on as he wrapped his arms around her.

He was her rock. This was where she was meant to be.

She wasn't even sure where the unsettled feeling had come from, or the mixed-up thoughts.

She turned her head and pressed her lips to his cheek. "Nothing's wrong," she repeated before sitting up to cup his cheek with her hand. "Consider it a mental challenge I'm untangling. I *know* I'm valued. I'm very happy I could step in and help at the clinic when Sharon needed to deal with her mom being sick. I adored helping Tamara when she was pregnant—taking care of the family and spending time with Sasha and Emma gave me a chance to create some amazing memories. I wouldn't have given that up for the world."

Josiah continued to look thoughtful. "But you're right. You helped her and then Sonora with the animal shelter. Then you moved in with me, and ever since then you've—" Lisa could all but see the gears turning in his brain before his gaze widened. "You've gone from one place to the next, one sister or friend to the next, helping everybody along the way without ever asking for payment or reward. You're amazing."

A laugh escaped her. "I love you. I wasn't looking for pats on the back, and I mean that. Although it's awfully nice to get them."

"I can't believe I never noticed." He tucked his fingers under her chin and raised her face to his. "I guess I'm guilty for not encouraging you to get a nine-to-five. I like having you around as much as possible. I like that I can take care of you."

"The fact you have ample money from your trust fund has made a difference," Lisa admitted.

Not having to worry about how to pay the bills was a glorious freedom, and she knew exactly how privileged that made her. Which is why having a grumbly brain was extra annoying.

"Like I said before, this is nothing bad, but it's something that's been on my mind since the beginning of the year. I need to figure out exactly what I want for a job title that's going to make me feel as if I've accomplished..."

She paused. Dammit—she wasn't going to blow smoke up her own skirt, but she'd accomplished a hell of a lot over the years on a regular basis.

Lisa shook her head but gave him a wink. "And that's not even the real issue, so I should probably shut up and think about this a bit more."

Josiah kissed her, soft and sweet. "You need somebody to throw ideas at, I'm here. And if you just want somebody to tell you that you're awesome, I'm fully on board for that as well."

"You are a darling man," she whispered.

She was about to give him a kiss in return when Ollie went off like an alarm system. The bratty little beast raced back and forth between where Lisa and Josiah sat and the front door, yipping at high-volume.

"Ollie," the two of them said sternly.

Lisa was up, headed for the door. "More emus?"

She stepped carefully around Ollie, who was losing her mind with excitement.

Josiah got a glimpse out the front window first. "Oh, hell. Stay back from the door," he ordered. He hurried down the hallway toward his office, calling over his shoulder, "That's a caribou. Don't open the door until I've got the rifle."

She gaped after him before turning her attention back on the massive creature headed directly for their front stairs. "You're going to *shoot* it? What the heck is a caribou doing in our yard? Where are these animals coming from?"

Once again, Lisa moved to contain the barking fury that was their pet. This time, she sat and pulled Ollie's body harness on so she had something concrete to clasp when the dog tried to wiggle away.

The pup wasn't trying to hurt anyone, but she was definitely out of sorts, still barking desperately.

Josiah was back, rifle in hand. "I don't plan to shoot it unless I have to," he told Lisa. "But that's a lady caribou, and with the rack she's wearing, there's no way to be sure she won't hurt somebody if she decides to attack."

Lisa caught the weapon firmly when he held it out, waiting as he pulled on his thick winter jacket. "The ladies have the antlers? I didn't know that."

"They both get antlers, but the guys drop them in the fall after mating season is over. The ladies keep them so that they can fight for food to make sure their babies grow enough to survive after being born in the spring."

"Sweet," Lisa said. "They're like the Amazons of the ungulate kingdom."

As she hoped, her veterinarian snickered. "Something like that. Keep hold of Ollie, will you?"

She squeezed his arm with her free hand as he took the weapon from her. "Be careful, my brave knight."

He flashed her a grin that said he was more than a little proud that she called him that, even in passing.

Ollie only calmed down once Lisa took her into the back bedroom, leaving her tucked safely behind the door so she could get her own coat on and cautiously head outside to see what was happening.

Josiah was already walking back toward the house.

He waved her over. "There's a whole herd of them. I convinced our visitor to return to her family. As soon as she joined them, the herd took off at high speed to the south onto crown land."

Lisa peered back the way he was pointing. "We don't usually get caribou in this part of the world, do we?"

He shook his head. "And I don't think this is like the emu. No way is anybody keeping an entire herd of caribou as pets."

"Well, somebody's gotta know where they came from."

"We'll track them down eventually." He caught her by the hand. "Now that it's safe, want to go for a walk with me, Ms. Coleman?"

"I would love to, Mr. Ryder." She snuggled into his side, wrapping her arm around his elbow. "I love mornings like these. Crisp and cold. Every breath tastes as if I just pipelined an energy shot straight into my veins."

He glanced around. "Where's Ollie?"

"I locked her up," Lisa confessed. "I didn't think it was safe to have her rushing to defend us when there were animals with battering rams on their heads wandering around."

"Good idea. I'll put away the rifle and grab her. We can go for a nice long walk. She'd like that as well."

An hour later, Lisa had pushed aside all of the annoyances nagging at her. What did it matter that she'd never had an official job? She had an amazing guy, and she had a pet who adored her.

Or maybe it was the guy who adored her, she thought with a snicker, glancing up to discover Josiah once again staring at her.

"You keep looking at me like that, and this walk is going to get derailed really quickly," she warned.

"You say that as if it's a bad thing," Josiah murmured.

Having the day off meant not just enjoying their lazy winter walk but a chance to do a few other things that Lisa wanted to. After lunch with Josiah, she headed over to Karen's to pick up the box of photos that the Whiskey Creek girls had promised to go through. Together they needed to find materials and write up some stories for a joint Coleman clan project.

The undertaking was something the cousins back in Rocky Mountain House had come up with. Lisa had no problem helping, but it was kind of nice that for the first time ever, she wasn't attempting to work behind the scenes to coordinate what was going on.

Which meant she had time to explore an idea of her own. Using some of the past history that was being shared amongst all the cousins, Lisa was putting together a small scrapbook for Julia. An opportunity for their youngest sister to find out more about where she came from.

Lisa laughed at herself. Even when she kept out of the main coordinating, she was still organizing something. It was hard for a leopard to change its spots.

She knocked on the door then let herself in. "Karen?"

No answer. She checked her phone to find a message.

Karen: *Sorry. Had to run over to Tamara's to grab something. Make yourself comfy. I'll be right back.*

Lisa didn't bother to respond. She took her sister at her

word, and after rummaging in the refrigerator to grab an iced tea, she settled on the couch next to where half the contents of a box was already spread over the coffee table.

Ollie jumped up beside her, followed immediately by the sweet white kitten by the name of Dandelion Fluff. Dandy and Ollie touched noses before the kitten firmly made his way into Lisa's lap. He stretched for a moment, his little pink nose wiggling.

Lisa brushed two fingers down the back of his head. "Well, aren't you cuddly today?"

Dandy curled up directly on top of her stomach, a small, round bundle of fluff. An instant later, Ollie had settled in as well, torso draped over Lisa's thighs so she could rest her chin on the back of the cat and still crack open an eye every now and then to make sure her human wasn't going anywhere.

Lisa snickered at discovering she was trapped. The coffee table was only a foot away, but there was no way to grab anything off it without disturbing the very relaxed creatures in her lap.

"Well, I suppose that's one way to make me take some R & R." Lisa eased her head back on the couch and took a deep breath. The peaceful quiet of Karen's home surrounded her, with nothing but a grandfather clock ticking somewhere in the background.

Unbelievably, she must've fallen asleep, because the next thing she knew, Ollie had gone off again. For a well-behaved little dog, the creature had suddenly decided to exercise her vocal cords far more than Lisa thought appropriate.

Ollie's bark went off in Dandy's ear. The cat leapt skyward, an annoyed yowl escaping him. He landed on the floor, shooting to the side of the room as Ollie jumped off the couch as well, beelining instead for the front door, where Karen stood.

"Ollie. Be quiet." Lisa attempted to blink herself awake.

Karen glowered at the barking dog as if she'd discovered a pile of poop instead of a pile of pup at her feet. "Every now and then I remember why I don't usually like animals in the house."

"Oh, stop it," Lisa said with a laugh, crossing the room quickly. The instant she scooped up Ollie, the dog ceased her annoying new habit. "I have no idea what's gotten into her."

Dandy was perched on top of the nearest bookcase, and he hissed his disapproval at all the noise and upheaval.

Karen snickered. "Well, it seems as if the animal kingdom is out of sorts. Come on, we'll grab them some treats and sweet talk them into loving us again."

The pets settled, and Lisa enjoyed her time with her sister. Relaxation lingered all the way home, or at least until she cracked open the front door and Ollie rushed in to immediately begin barking again.

"Beast. *Stop* it." Lisa followed her to discover Josiah balancing on one leg as he worked the bootjack. "Hey. You just get home?"

He nodded, snapping his fingers at Ollie and pointing at the floor. "Sit."

Ollie sat instantly, but she kept yipping at him.

Josiah grunted in annoyance. "Damn. I was out with the emu. She probably smells him on me."

"Grab a shower," Lisa suggested, holding Ollie in place until Josiah had both stockinged feet firmly on the floor.

"Come join me." Josiah's blue eyes sparkled.

Which seemed like a fantastic idea on all sorts of levels. Lisa flashed him a grin. "Give me five. Ollie is not invited to this party."

"Poor pup."

"Consequences," Lisa said dryly.

"Yup. And there's a reward for good behavior." His grin widened. "I'll go warm up the water. Don't take too long."

CHAPTER 4

Josiah stepped into the veterinary office, pleased as punch to offer a solution to one of their recent mysteries. "You know, we're lucky we only had emus and caribou in the yard."

Before Lisa could look up from her desk, Ollie sprinted out from behind the counter, teeth bared and hackles up. She wasn't barking, but she was definitely not happy to see him.

Their pet's unusual behavior was growing stronger and more worrisome.

"There's something worse?" Lisa stood, bringing him back to what he'd come to share.

"A bunch of fences went down at the conservation farm the Calgary Zoo runs by De Winton. They had a mass escape last week, including emus and the caribou. We didn't get the whooping cranes, though."

"That's too funny. Glad we can help get at least one home safe." Lisa moved toward him, arms open for a hug.

Ollie stepped between them, lowered her head, and snarled.

Josiah stopped where he was. "She been like this all morning?"

Lisa sighed as she snapped a lead on Ollie's collar, guiding her back behind the desk. The little beast splayed her legs out and braced as if she had to maintain that patch of ground.

"Sort of? She stopped barking but started growling at anyone who came near." Lisa's expression grew more concerned. "But yeah, she's off. This isn't her."

He met Lisa's gaze straight on. "Let me give her an examination. Maybe she's coming down with something. You're right, this isn't her, and if there's something we can do to stop her from being so upset, we should do it."

Lisa snapped the lead to the wall, which kept Ollie secured within a three-foot radius of the reception desk. Then she came out to give Josiah a hug. "Office is closed for the rest of the day. Do you want me to help you with her exam, or do you mind if I head over to Tamara's?"

He leaned their foreheads together. "Probably easier if I do the exam by myself. Having only one person poking and prodding at her might stop Ollie from getting as worked up. You want me to pick something up for supper? Since you've been toiling in my office all day?"

She wrinkled her nose, considering. "Sure. Whatever you want, though. I'm not really hungry."

He kissed her, ignoring the rumble rising from the corner that said Ollie was still highly pissed off about something.

Lisa grabbed her purse and headed out.

Josiah waited until the door closed and locked it after her to slowly approach Ollie. "Hey, sweetness. What's up with you? You not feeling very good?"

He squatted a few feet away, looking over the little terrier with a lot more concern than he'd allowed Lisa to see. When an animal changed their character so completely for no good reason, it usually meant trouble.

Ollie tilted her head to the side and examined Josiah. Paws

in front of her, she rose, and her little tail began wagging. Slow at first and then hard enough that her entire body vibrated.

That was more typical.

Josiah out held his fingers. Ollie gave them a sniff and then a lick. Vibrating so hard now that she was about to rock off her feet.

"Silly beast." Josiah unhooked the lead and led her into an examining room. He may as well do a full workup to find out if there was something wrong.

It was as if he had two dogs. One, their usual Ollie, sweet and loving. The animal that let him examine her—including taking blood samples—without ever a woof of disapproval.

The other? Was the minute terror who showed up the instant they walked back in the door at home.

Ollie had slept on the trip back to the ranch with her chin on Josiah's thigh. Now five steps into the house, she whirled and once again bared her teeth at him.

"Anything?" Lisa asked from where she stood in the doorway of the kitchen.

"I put the blood work in for testing tomorrow, but as far as I can tell, she's perfectly fine."

"Okay. Then if she keeps this up, she's going to get used to spending more time in the doghouse." Lisa didn't look thrilled about it, but she shrugged. "Otherwise known as the guest bathroom. Did you grab supper?"

He held up a bag. "The mighty hunter returns."

But even as they settled in for a meal and the rest of their evening, Josiah kept pondering what was going on and hoped like hell the test results would help show them something they could do.

Ollie was family, and having her out of sorts? It meant their world wasn't right.

Lisa's final day at the veterinary clinic was over and done.

She hated to admit that she was glad. Maybe working on a full-time basis was something you could get out of the habit for. She couldn't remember work ever making her this tired, not even while running around after her nieces 24/7.

She was definitely coming down with something. She didn't think she had a cold, and it was nothing she could put her finger on. Maybe she was dealing with an attack of laziness, because getting out of bed was the last thing she wanted to do.

Thank goodness for Saturday mornings. A teeny bit of guilt slipped in at how happy she was when Josiah woke at his usual early time but left her after one sweet, lingering kiss.

Nope. Screw the guilt. Lisa rolled into the warm spot he'd left behind, sprawling across the bed as she gloried in how comfortable it was.

When she finally got up, there was a note on the kitchen table for her.

Gone to Silver Stone. Back by lunch. Come join me if you want—Kelli wants me to take a look at Molasses.

Lisa checked the clock on the wall. Ten o'clock. There was still time to make it out there if she grabbed a quick breakfast. She poured herself a cup of coffee and stuck it in the microwave. She'd just hit the start button when the doorbell went off.

Her sister Julia stood on the other side of the door, gazing toward the sky as she waited.

Ollie, of course, was barking her head off.

"Just a minute. I've got to deal with the dog," Lisa called over the yapping.

"No problem."

Minutes later the barking continued, but it was contained in the guest bath. Julia was in the kitchen, paper bag in hand.

"I didn't know you were coming over," Lisa said. "Can I get you something?"

Julia shook her head. "I come bearing gifts." The microwave dinged, and she tipped her chin toward it. "You got something in there?"

"Yeah. Just a sec." Lisa opened the door and brought out the cup of warmed coffee. It looked pretty unappetizing, to be honest. She sniffed and tried not to gag. "Man, the cream must've gone off."

She dumped it down the sink, rinsing the cup and placing it in the drainer rack before facing her sister.

Julia no longer looked thoughtful. Julia was wearing a smirk.

Lisa folded her arms over her chest. "What?"

"Between that"—Julia pointed down the hallway to where Ollie continued to bark—"and that"—she pointed at the discarded coffee—"I think you need this."

The paper bag was thrust toward her.

It only took a second to undo the rolled top and grab the box inside.

Lisa froze. "Why did you get me a pregnancy test?" It didn't take but a second for one plus one to add up to three. "Oh *shit*."

"It's just a guess," Julia said. "But you mentioned Ollie's weird behaviour and how the change came on really suddenly. I know how much Ollie loves Josiah, so it can't be that those feelings vanished overnight."

Great big enormous bubbles were churning in Lisa's gut, and it had nothing to do with sniffing rancid coffee. "How could I be pregnant?"

A snort escaped Julia.

She wiped at her mouth and tried to cover it up. "Well. It goes like this. When a man loves a woman very, very much—"

"Shut up," Lisa said, amusement trickling in despite her shocked nerves. "I know the mechanics," she offered dryly. "There've been no equipment failures."

With a huge sweep of her arm, Julia gestured down the hallway. "Take the test before you start worrying about when or how. I could be wrong, you know."

Only now that the idea had been presented to her, Lisa couldn't believe she'd missed the signs.

"I'm going to wait, if you don't mind." She wiggled the box in the air. "This is something I'd like to do with Josiah. No matter what it says."

Her sister's smile deepened. "No problem. But just so you know, if you are pregnant, you made me fifty bucks."

Lisa laughed out loud. "Hey, I'm the one with the reputation for betting about anything and everything. Who's going to accuse me of corrupting you?"

"Kelli at Silver Stone." Julia motioned toward the table. "Come on. You said you would tell me about summer camp out in Rocky Mountain House. It sounded as if you guys had a lot of fun back then."

Which is how Lisa lasted until Josiah came home. Although, by the laughter in Julia's eyes when she left the house an hour later, chances were that some of the stories Lisa had told had paused in the wrong places or completely cut off before they were finished as distraction rolled in.

A great, big, enormous distraction.

Josiah wasn't even all the way through the door when Lisa confronted him. "I think I know what's wrong with Ollie."

The worry in his eyes faded to shock as she described her morning with Julia.

Three minutes later they stood by the edge of the counter in the bathroom, staring down at the pregnancy test kit. Lisa slid under his arm a little tighter. Josiah squeezed, silently watching with her as two solid pink lines appeared.

Lisa swallowed hard. The tumbling in her stomach had continued, but now every single one of her organs was working overtime. Her heart pounded, her brain whirled, and every inch of her skin felt electrified.

She turned to Josiah. "Wow."

He caught her fingers and pressed a kiss to her knuckles. "Are you okay with this?"

"Are you?" Lisa examined his face, but all she saw there was a damn actor. Holding back. Waiting to find out what she wanted before sharing what he felt inside.

To hell with it. The truth burst free like a million butterflies rushing out onto the wind "I am really, really excited—"

Before she could finish speaking, he picked her up and damn near whirled her, a shout rising from his lips that set Ollie barking again, the rumble echoing from the other side of the wall where the poor puppy was once again contained in the other bathroom.

"Yes. I'm okay with this," Josiah declared. "I am really, *really* okay with this. It's just we've never talked about kids. Well, not about having them yet."

"I think we didn't talk about them because we figured they'd happen someday." He'd stopped spinning her, which was good, because the room still whirled.

Josiah settled on the edge of the bed, and she knelt over him, torso to torso so she could hold on tight.

He nuzzled against her neck. "Someday is now. That's pretty amazing."

"Someday is nine months from now." She put a hand between them and pushed so she could gaze into his face. "When did this happen? We used condoms."

His shoulders lifted. "Does it really matter?"

"Just for calculating due dates." She shivered as those words registered on her brain. "Oh. My. God."

Josiah looked a little dazed as well. "That just made it seem a little more real," he confessed.

"A due date. For a baby." Lisa tried the words on for size. "For *our* baby. The start of our family."

He pressed his hands to her cheeks, his expression full of wonder. When he sat there, staring, it was a little bit humbling, and felt like a whole lot of heart squeezing.

"I love you," she whispered.

He dipped his chin. "I love you," he repeated. His gaze drifted down her body to land on her belly. He pressed his fingers against her waist. "And I love you too."

That was it. Lisa lost it.

Fortunately, Josiah wasn't scared off by a few tears, which was a good thing, because being pregnant and all, who knew what hormonal adventure she was about to get up to.

A baby. Wow.

By the time she pulled herself together, Josiah slid her onto the mattress then motioned for her to stay put. "Now that we know what's up, I bet we can deal with Ollie."

The yipping in the background had faded to one long howl every fifteen seconds, but as the door opened, the cream-coloured dog shot into the room and somehow managed to launch herself onto the bed.

She covered Lisa with kisses, eyeing Josiah with suspicion as he reentered the room.

"I can't believe it. She knew I was pregnant." Lisa sighed as Ollie growled softly. "What are you going to do?"

"I'll move slowly. Hopefully she'll get over being this protective at some point, but right now, you've got yourself a guardian doggy." He stepped around her to the other side of Ollie, carefully settling so he could pet the puppy without getting too close to Lisa.

Ollie's tail waggled just the slightest bit even as she pushed against Lisa and kept a careful eye on Josiah.

Nine months, minus however many days. Dealing with an overprotective guard dog was going to be only part of the adventure.

Lisa couldn't wait.

CHAPTER 5

September 5th weekend, second wedding day for Zach and Julia

Josiah adored every inch of Lisa, and the changes happening slowly but steadily over the past months had only enhanced the things he loved in the first place. Not talking about the physical changes, although he was more than willing to admit that her pregnant body was sexier than he had ever imagined.

Her confidence had risen even higher. He couldn't get enough of watching her strut her stuff as they prepared for Julia and Zach's wedding.

As masses of family descended on Red Boot ranch, the Whiskey Creek Coleman sisters and the horde of Zach's female relatives had contributed to the mischief in equal portions.

But as they made it through the wedding ceremony, and the gift opening, and all of the other planned activities, it was having Lisa at his side that made Josiah the happiest.

They rested for a moment during the dance, seated beside Tamara Stone, who held her nearly year-and-a-half-old son.

Tyler squirmed, the toddler wiggling with way too much energy for this time of night.

"Let me take him," Josiah offered.

Tamara handed the boy over immediately. "Have at 'im, Uncle Josiah." She glanced at Lisa and shook her head. "You look so damn good. I looked like a house when I was at your stage of pregnancy."

"Bullshit," Lisa returned. "You barely gained any weight, you were so sick the entire time. I'm way bigger than you were, and I still have nearly eight weeks to go."

"I'm glad you didn't get the nonstop nausea." Tamara dipped her chin then grinned. "Although I'll admit I'm also glad you had the decency to throw up a little during the first three months."

"You would have never forgiven me if I breezed through the entire pregnancy," Lisa drawled. "I'm much too smart for that."

Tamara turned to Josiah. "So. Today give you and Lisa any ideas?"

"*Tamara.*" Lisa folded her arms over her chest and raised a brow. "I know. Let's talk about when you and Caleb are going to get started on another playmate for Tyler and our kiddo."

Tamara narrowed her gaze. "Now, that's just nasty."

Josiah snickered and spoke seriously to the kid in his arms, who was happily playing with the keys Josiah had handed him. "See, Tyler? Having a sister is an awesome thing. And you've got two already."

He was kind of happy to have avoided the discussion, though. He was telling the truth when he said marriage wasn't that high a priority for him.

Only, watching Zach and Julia take their vows—it *had* tweaked something inside. While Josiah wasn't looking to get married, he wouldn't say no to it either. His parents had been married for umpteen years, and his sisters, both of whom had tied the knot, all shared good memories of the event.

He wished he cared a little more or a little less, but the truth was that he was so exactly in limbo, there was no use putting more energy into deciding why the topic kept coming to mind.

Fortunately, he had the most wonderful source of distraction in the woman who, while not his by name, was definitely his in every other way possible.

He and Lisa headed back to the ranch house after the dancing was over. Lisa sat in the middle seat of the truck, arms wrapped around his biceps, her head leaning against his shoulder.

For a second, he thought he heard her snore. "You headed for lights-out already?" he teased softly.

"Pregnant lady is tired," she murmured back. "That was a beautiful wedding. I'm so happy for Julia."

"Zach as well. I thought he was going to break something in his face, he was grinning so hard."

"His little sister is crack. I'm serious. I need to find Petra somebody here in town, because she would fit in just fine with us Whiskeyteers."

He didn't bother to try and hide his chuckle of amusement. Just started singing the matchmaker song from *Fiddler on the Roof*, emphasizing all the men who were absolutely terrible.

The snickering started as he sang in a falsetto voice, her amusement turning into actual gasps of laughter by the time he pulled into the parking space outside their house.

"Stop. You're killing me," Lisa wheezed.

He swept her into his arms, nudging the truck door shut with his hip before carrying her toward the front stairs. "My singing's not *that* bad."

She tangled her arms around his neck and offered him a sweet, sleepy smile. "True. Ollie's not even barking yet."

Although the little terrier was waiting for them just inside the door. She still snarled momentarily at Josiah until Lisa dropped to her knees and offered reassurance that everything was fine.

The next morning Lisa wore her most dangerous expression.

"I have something I want you to do for me today," she informed him while they were still at the breakfast table.

"Before or after the family lunch today?"

"Right after breakfast, if you don't mind. It's nothing too big, but it's something I need your help with."

Only, once they'd cleaned up the kitchen and headed up to the loft as requested, Josiah gaped in surprise. "Your idea of what's not too big and important is little out of whack with mine," he informed her.

Lisa stood beside the mattress on the floor, a wide beam of sunlight dancing over her skin. She'd stripped to nothing but her bra and a pair of panties—*thong* panties, if his guess was correct.

She planted her fists on her hips. "Is that a crack about my pregnant belly?" she demanded.

He crossed the room instantly, curling his hands gently over the warm skin of that amazing part of her. "Definitely not. But, sweetheart, me taking naked pictures of you falls into the category of something that's very important. Just so you know."

She cuddled against him, her scent wrapping around him and making him happy. "I love the pictures we took during that girls' night out."

He loved them too. "*Oui, mon amour. Tu étais magnifique.*"

Lisa grinned. "I felt very sexy, and very happy I could take those pictures and share them with you. But now I want some pictures that are very much for me. Do you mind?"

He looked down at her, this woman who had stepped into his life with the force of a hurricane. Everything she touched turned to gold. Everything she did for him made him that much more shocked that he'd survived so many years without the heart now beating in his chest.

"I'm very privileged to take the pictures, but trust me. These are for me as well."

The number one thing running through his brain as Lisa slipped off the rest of her clothes and proceeded to pose with her hands barely covering her breasts, angling so the sweet swell of her belly featured prominently in some shots—

Thank goodness for digital cameras.

If they'd done this in the old days, he would've had to learn how to use a dark room so he could have developed them on his own. No way in hell was anyone else seeing her like this. She was an earth mother. She was a goddess.

She was *his*.

Many fascinating minutes later, Lisa had reached the point where she was stretched out on the mattress, head tilted, hair cascading to the ground behind her. She arched her back, her heavy breasts lifted, one knee bent upward. She was a Madonna and a seductress at the same time.

He snapped another couple shots then joined her.

"Let me see," she said, eagerly reaching for his phone.

Josiah tossed the phone to the floor, sliding it over the carpet and out of reach. "Pictures later. Right now, I have some worshiping to do."

Her expression lit up, and she glanced up from under lashes that had suddenly gone heavy. "This sounds rather time-consuming."

"If I'm doing it right, neither of us will care if we don't get anything else done today."

Which was how they almost missed the post-wedding family luncheon. The pictures on his phone, however, made the teasing they received totally worthwhile.

The second-best moment after the lovemaking was when his out-of-the-blue idea turned into a perfect gift for Lisa. He took his favourite picture—the one where he'd propped up his phone and set the timer then *he'd* cradled her belly, fingers and thumbs forming the shape of a heart over the swell—and turned it into a card that said *I Love You Two*.

She cried for a minute when she opened it, shaking her head as if in disbelief, but the joy in her eyes when she finally lifted her tear-filled gaze to his was real. "You are amazing."

"I had good material to work with."

Another day. Another step closer to the next adventure.

CHAPTER 6

October 6, pre-Thanksgiving Weekend

L isa pressed her fists against her hips and glared at Josiah. "We already talked about this. I don't know why you're trying to change things at the last minute."

Josiah was wearing his reasonable face. The one that had begun to show up a lot more often as her belly got bigger and her balance grew worse.

She didn't like it. His face. The belly and the shitty balance were part and parcel of the baby gig, but him humouring her? Not on her happy making chart.

"Yes," he said with a slow nod. "We agreed that we'd attend the Coleman party in Rocky Mountain House. But that was before the weatherman announced there's the potential for a huge snowstorm to arrive this weekend, in spite of it being early October."

"It's not as if we haven't had snow in October before," Lisa pointed out.

"No, that's true. Only we've never had to drive in a snowstorm when one of us is a pregnant lady with two weeks to go until she pops. And the other one of us is a future father who is not eager to deliver said baby on the side of the highway if we have vehicle problems in the middle of an out-of-season snowstorm."

"Use your reasonable tone of voice on me again, and I will sic Ollie on you," Lisa threatened.

"*Ha.* Ollie and I have come to an arrangement. Both of us think it's better for you, for *all* of us, to stay home." Josiah made his point by giving a little whistle.

The pup showed up, rushing from where she'd been settled in the kitchen. Instantly, she pulled a sheepdog imitation and attempted to herd Lisa back into the bedroom. They had no idea why Ollie had decided to start doing this over the past couple days, but Josiah found it amusing as all get out.

Lisa? Not so much.

"I don't approve of this new habit of hers," Lisa complained, but she reached for Josiah's hand then tucked herself into his arms.

"It's better than growling or baring her teeth."

True, and he'd put up with a lot of that over the past months without complaining about how unreasonable it was that Ollie seemed to love Lisa better right now.

"I wanted to go to the party," she said with an exaggerated whine and a pout on her lips.

He pressed a kiss to her temple, holding her tight. "I know, sweetie. But please? So I don't have to worry?"

That was the nail in the coffin. Lisa had no intention of pushing for something that was going to potentially hurt him. No matter how much fun the party would have been.

Which was part of what they'd been doing over the past months—continuing to learn how to be a couple. Learning how much being together required give-and-take. Making it clear when something was important to one of them, and letting things slide when they were lower on the priority scale.

Now with only a short time left before they were a couple plus one, Lisa realized all over again how much her heart belonged to this man. "I love you."

He tapped his fingers against her chest and then against her baby bump. "I love you two."

She knew exactly what he was saying. What he meant. Emotion welled up, and suddenly none of it was enough.

She wanted more.

Lisa looked up at him, tears pooling at the back of her eyes. "Okay. We won't risk heading out to Rocky for the party. But I'd like to do something special here. Before my sisters leave, if you don't mind."

"That's a great idea." He swayed them slightly, rocking gently in a silent dance. "What do you want to do that's going to make you happy?"

Her idea was the culmination of months of pondering, mixed with the high-voltage, high-test trust that had continued to grow with each sweet and tender moment of Josiah sharing his unconditional love.

Her idea was slightly off-the-wall—

No, it was *wildly* unexpected, but even as she stared into Josiah's eyes, Lisa knew this was the moment. "I want us to get married."

Josiah's jaw dropped. Damn near bounced off the floor, in fact, but then he was moving. Once again, he twirled her in a circle, the word *yes* echoing from his lips before he put her down and kissed her senseless.

Although it was difficult to kiss when they were both grinning that hard.

He finally backed up just far enough to meet her gaze. "You're serious?"

"Uh-huh. Friday night? We can have everybody over for dinner and then get it done before they leave Saturday."

"Not that I don't believe you, but I'm going to do one final check, because every time until now when getting married has been mentioned, you've been very firmly against it." He braced as if preparing for impact. "This isn't a hormone thing, is it?"

She snickered even as she tapped the side of her fist against his biceps. "Dangerous move, but I get why you're wondering." She tugged him toward her favourite spot in the living room. They'd discovered if he took the corner of the couch and she curled up mostly on top of him, her belly rested against his body and made both of them happy.

Ollie jumped up by their feet and settled in place, pinning them so there was no retreat. The puppy had finally accepted Josiah as a necessary evil.

Lisa stroked her hand along Josiah's strong jawline as she shared the truth. "I've spent a lot of time this year trying to figure out what the weird missing thing is that's been bugging me. It's not as if there was any job that I really wanted to apply for or a professional designation that seemed important enough to label myself with. It's only the last little while that it finally sank in hard what I was really looking for."

"Go on." He trapped her fingers and held them against his chest.

"I want a label that is absolutely my decision. I've been a cowgirl, and a sister, and a helper, and so much more. All those things were the right thing to do. They called to a part of my nature, and they made me happy." A little set of feet shoved against her ribs hard enough to make her gasp. "Oh, boy. Kiddo's doing gymnastics."

She slid Josiah's hand over the active part of her belly, and they waited. Only a second later, she sucked in a breath, and

Josiah laughed. "It's a good thing you don't have too much longer to go. Our little cowboy's already got their boots on."

Looking at his hand gently touching her belly. Caring for their baby before they had even arrived—Lisa looked up at Josiah and finished her thought the best she could. "Even me being a mom and us starting our family just happened. And I'm glad for that, but I want us to do one thing because we deliberately choose it. I want a label that I pick, and it's your name. I want to be a Ryder. Maybe it's silly, but us having one last name that we share so we can both give it to this baby seems right."

The love shining in Josiah's eyes was staggeringly intense. "I have never been so proud," he confessed. "Not just because you've chosen to take my name but because you're saying what I've done over the years is valuable enough to make my name mean something."

His voice cracked at the end before he went silent.

He caught the back of her head and pressed it against his chest, and while she couldn't see his face, she was pretty sure she wasn't the only one crying right now.

When they told her sisters, there were more happy tears. Also shouting, and laughter, and a whole lot of teasing.

Her father hurriedly made the trip down from Rocky Mountain House to join them, and only three days later, on the Friday night before Thanksgiving, they gathered in a room full of people. Video monitors were set up around the perimeter, each holding a link to Josiah's scattered family so they could take part in the festivities as well.

Lisa stood next to Julia, pointing everybody out. "Lenora is in L.A. And that's Micah in New York. You remember him. He's the one who got us the show tickets for Vegas last year."

Julia wiggled her fingers at Josiah's brother. "One of my favourite cities," she teased.

In the end, Malachi Fields, family friend and local justice of the peace, had to tap a spoon on a glass to get everybody's attention so he could start the ceremony. "I'd let you continue the party," the tall, elegant man said, his smile flashing brightly as he glanced around the room. "But if we don't actually let them say the proper bits and pieces, there'll be nothing to celebrate."

"In this family, there's always something to celebrate," Tamara offered.

The room finally settled down, and suddenly it was happening. No big fancy gown or decorated hall. Just her and Josiah, rising from where they'd been placed next to each other at the table. Ollie sat obediently with her butt on Lisa's foot.

Surrounded by family, surrounded by friends.

Maybe they hadn't been travelling around the world. But there were people from around the world looking on with love and sending good wishes their way as Josiah took her fingers in his.

Josiah focused tightly on her, lifting her knuckles to press a kiss to them before he began. "I made this for you."

He handed her a set of cards.

Lisa began to laugh. "Tell me you didn't try to script this." She glanced down and read quickly, a sharp burst of laughter escaping before she lifted the card higher and read out loud. "I was tempted to write a script but figured you'd improv anyway. We're on our own, sweetheart. I get to go first."

Laughter rumbled around the room.

Josiah's lips curled upward before he continued, "Spontaneous is the way it should be. Because never knowing from one minute to the next what you're going to do makes this thing between us fresh every day. Looking up to see mischief in your eyes makes me feel alive and ready to take on the world."

His gaze drifted to her belly. She wore a soft-blue long-sleeve shirt that stretched over the roundness between them.

Josiah adjusted his position slightly so he could wrap an arm around her and press a hand over where their baby rested. Then he lifted his gaze to hers once again. "I love you, Lisa. I'm so glad you want to take my name. I'm so humbled that you want to spend the rest of your life with me. I plan to do everything I can to make you happy."

Wow. She swallowed hard, but the huge knot in her throat refused to go away.

"I had no idea this was going to be so difficult," she confessed, voice wavering. Totally shaken to her roots by everything he'd said. "You do make me happy. And I do want to spend my life with you. And I think you're the best man in the entire world, which means taking your name is a no-brainer."

His grin flashed.

Lisa lifted her chin. "And I've probably not said it often enough, or loud enough, or enough times without using words, but I'll keep working on that going forward. I love you, Josiah. I *adore* you. I'm so glad you're mine."

There might've been a bit after with the justice of the peace and signing papers, but all Lisa saw was Josiah's eyes. The love in them. The smile on his lips, the feel of his strong arm around her as he held on tight.

The bit she did remember with complete clarity? Malachi's final announcement. "I'm very pleased to present Dr. and Mrs. Josiah and Lisa Ryder."

The room erupted into cheers and noisemakers. Josiah's fingers tightened around her hip, and bubbles of happiness flitted through her bloodstream as if she'd been mainlining champagne.

The party carried on, but Lisa eventually caught Josiah by the hand and brought him with her down the hallway to the privacy of their bedroom. Ollie was all but tangled under their feet the entire way.

"Are we done partying?" Josiah asked with a smile.

"I'm done," she confessed. "But they're all having a good time. No need for them to stop. Come tuck me into bed?"

"Just let me tell Zach to lock up for us. He and Julia can shut down the place."

She'd barely finished brushing her teeth and getting ready for bed when he was back. A moment later, he slid between the sheets and wrapped his arms around her. Spooning her close against his body, nuzzling against the back of her neck. His big hand splayed over the swell of her belly. "Thank you for a wonderful evening."

Sleep was sneaking in. "It's what I wanted too, remember?"

"I'm still the luckiest guy in the world," Josiah informed her briskly. "Now go to sleep, Mrs. Ryder. I want to fool around with my wife tomorrow, and she needs a lot of rest these days."

"Wow." Lisa took a deep breath. "I'm no longer a Coleman. I'm a Ryder."

He chuckled. "I love you. Go to sleep."

"I love you too."

It wasn't that big of a change, but it was, in all the ways that were really important. He was her husband. She was his wife.

She had a new last name.

It had been a good day.

CHAPTER 7

The wedding had been everything he'd hoped for.

All of Lisa's family heading out to the Coleman party in Rocky Mountain House without them early the very next day? Not what he'd hoped for.

She didn't say anything, but the *looks* Lisa gave him? They got even worse when the sun came out, shining as if Mother Nature herself were sticking out her tongue at Josiah, just to get him in trouble.

"Wow. Sure looks as if a nasty snowstorm is on the way," Lisa said as she leaned back in her chair and propped her feet up on Josiah's lap. "Dangerous-looking weather. So glad we didn't venture out into it."

"Looking for trouble?" Josiah offered blandly.

Lisa let her head flop to the side. "I'm *bored*. There's nothing to do." She eyed him speculatively. "We could still go to the party, you know."

"*Lisa*." He lifted her feet off his lap, tickling the bottom of her foot before he let her go. "The whole reason they call it *weather* is because they don't know whether or not they can actually predict what's going to happen."

"Hardy har, har," she muttered.

"If you'd like, you can come along with me. I figured I could get a bunch of pro bono visits done today." He eyed her belly and then her bare feet. "It means you have to get dressed, *warmly*, and you have to promise to tell me if you get tired and want to come home."

Lisa damn near bounced out of her chair with excitement. Teacup abandoned, she hurried down the hallway toward their bedroom, calling over her shoulder, "I can be dressed in just a few minutes."

Josiah held his tongue. No way in hell was he going to tell her how cute she looked waddling down the hallway now that the weight of the baby had dropped.

In fact, he was pretty sure even thinking the word *waddling* was dangerous.

Still, she *was* cute. And his wife. His heart turned over once again when she came out wearing maternity jeans over the baby bump, tying the ends of one of his flannel shirts underneath.

He caught her close, unable to resist. "You are the sexiest damn woman, especially wearing my clothes."

She joined him in the kiss, body pressed against his, not as if she were trying to turn the moment sexual, but as if she were leaning into him because the connection gave them both strength.

Her belly tightened. He circled his palm slowly over the surface. "More Braxton Hicks?"

Lisa blew out a long, slow breath. "Off and on. I suppose I should be happy for a bit of practice before the big day, but damn, they hurt."

Maybe taking her with him wasn't the best idea. He glanced around at their warm cozy home and tried to think of something that would distract her enough that she would willingly volunteer to abandon their plans to wander.

"Oh, no, you don't." Lisa caught hold of the front of his shirt and shook him. "You've got that look in your eyes again. The one that says you'd like to surround me in Bubble Wrap."

"I can't stop thinking it," Josiah protested. "Doesn't mean I'm going to act on it."

"Damn right, you aren't." She stomped past him to the front door, doing a little dance as she attempted to slip her feet into her boots without any help, not being able to see her feet past the baby bump.

Josiah got down on his knees and guided her. Her hand rested on his shoulder and gave a gentle squeeze of thanks.

Fortunately, the first stop he planned to make was out at the animal rescue site.

They'd barely even entered the yard when Sonora Fallen was out of her house and waving Lisa over. "I know I saw you last night, but we didn't really get a chance to talk. Come, have a cup of tea with me," the youthful grandmother coaxed.

"Be right there," Lisa promised before turning to Josiah. "You're sneaky," she complained.

"I have no idea what you're talking about," Josiah said earnestly before kissing her nose and sending her on her way to the warm and comfortable house where he knew Sonora would keep an eye on Lisa and make sure she didn't overdo it.

Inside the shelter, he went to work checking the few animals that Sonora talked to him about the previous week. He was nearly done when an older man appeared at the edge of the workroom. The silver-haired man was the head foreman at the Silver Stone ranch. He was also sweet on Sonora, no matter how much they both protested.

Josiah was mighty curious what exactly Ashton Stewart was doing over at the animal shelter on such a regular basis. Josiah, Finn, and Zach had some ideas on the matter, but there was nothing specific they could tease the man about.

"Congratulations on your marriage." Ashton rested a hip on the table and gave a slow chin dip in Josiah's direction. "Wondered when you two would decide to make it official."

It was too tempting. "Didn't have to be official to be real," Josiah pointed out. "Two people who like to spend time together, who fit together pretty good as individuals into a couple—hard to call that anything but a permanent relationship."

Sadly, Ashton didn't take the bait. "Lisa still doing good? Everything all right with the baby?"

"She's up at the house with Sonora if you'd like to see her," Josiah offered. "I'm done here with the animals."

Ashton nodded approvingly. "I'll take you up on that."

There was no mistaking the delight in Lisa's eyes when he and Ashton entered the house. There was also no mistaking the flush that rose across Sonora's cheeks, but that one wasn't as easy to explain without dipping into territory Josiah didn't want to tread yet.

They all chatted for a while, Lisa's hand resting comfortably in Josiah's. He played with the ring he'd placed on her finger just the night before and wondered at how amazing life was.

Except for Lisa stiffening every now and then when the Braxton Hicks struck, her fingers squeezing around his hand, it was the kind of relaxing distraction he'd hoped to provide.

"You need to get anywhere quickly, or can I tempt you with some lunch?" Sonora pushed to her feet, gathering teacups.

Josiah looked at Lisa, who considered then nodded.

It was nearly two o'clock when they finally left the cozy home, Ashton lingering behind them.

It was quiet in the truck as they headed to the next location, at least until Lisa began to laugh softly. "Do those two really think that nobody knows what's going on?"

"That he likes her?" Josiah asked.

An inelegant snort escaped before Lisa turned laughing eyes

in his direction. "Oh, sweetie. Don't tell me you think those two are stuck at the innocent flirting stage. I bet they've been knocking boots for at least a year if not longer."

"*Lisa.*" Josiah was shocked for an instant until he really thought it through a little more. "Although, you know what? You're probably right."

"What's that? I didn't quite hear you."

"I said you're right—" It was his turn to roll his eyes. "Damn, you caught me. Again. Yes, those two are definitely getting up to mischief. Or they should be, considering the vibes they give off every time they're in each other's radius."

Lisa tangled her fingers around his arm, sighing as she leaned her head on him. "It's nice to know that thirty years from now, we'll still want to jump each other's bones."

He slowed, taking the corner cautiously. "I'm glad we won't have to sneak around corners to hook up."

"But sometimes we will," she informed him with a grin. "Because that will just make it even more fun."

Somehow he knew she was right about that as well.

Lisa leaned forward, hands cautiously wrapped over her belly as she peered out the window. "This is part of Lone Pine ranch, isn't it? Part of Brad and Hanna's land?"

"We're coming at it from the opposite side," Josiah told her. "That's why it doesn't look as familiar. Brad let the land to the Devereauxes, and they've got cattle here until the end of the month. François asked if I would check a few of their cows before they end up in the high hills where it's a lot more difficult to do an exam."

Lisa sighed happily. "I know where we're going. Hanna told me they put up a porch swing at the cabin. I will happily sit there while you go wrestle varmints."

Which made for another perfect part of the day. Lisa all bundled up and cozy on the porch swing, with pillows and a blanket he'd taken from the neat little cabin perched on the hillside.

Ollie would've normally spent the time following Josiah as he checked the animals, but she was one hundred percent convinced Lisa needed a foot warmer.

Glancing back at the cabin over and over as the afternoon passed was like sticking a cup under a running faucet. Every time Josiah saw her, a soft smile at her lips as she petted Ollie lazily and gazed over the countryside, his heart got a little fuller.

He was one animal away from being done when suddenly Ollie was at his feet. "Hey. You get bored of napping?"

Ollie danced a foot toward Lisa then back toward Josiah. Again, and again, as if she were a bee doing a dance to indicate this was the direction he really needed to go *right now*.

Or at least that's what became clear as Lisa pulled herself to a vertical seat on the porch swing, swearing loudly. "Josiah?"

He took off at a run, Ollie sprinting at his side. "What's up?"

Her eyes had gone wide, and she had both arms wrapped around her stomach. "I think my water just broke."

CHAPTER 8

Lisa was absolutely torn between laughing and cursing. Of course her water was going to break two weeks early, when none of her family was around, and she and Josiah were out in the middle of the bloody wilderness.

Then the pain hit, and she didn't have the breath to do anything except lift her gaze to Josiah's.

All things considered, if he'd cursed or looked the slightest bit panicked, she wouldn't have blamed him. But all trace of worry of any kind vanished, and the only thing she saw was competent excitement.

"Well, okay then. A little earlier than we expected, but I guess the bun in the oven is fully cooked." Josiah touched her cheek tenderly, even though she knew damn well he was also checking her pupils for dilation. "Let's get you in the truck. Remember, they said during prenatal classes that your water breaking isn't anything to worry about. We won't rush, but if we go now, we'll be on the highway before it's dark."

She nodded. "I guess they're not called Braxton Hicks anymore, are they?"

"You feeling them?"

The tightness of the band across her belly made it hard to take a deep breath. Combined with the fact that her lungs didn't seem to have enough room at the best of times, what with the baby consuming most of the room in her torso—

She gritted her teeth for a second, breathing shallowly.

His big palm landed on her back, and he rubbed it in circles, making soothing noises. "I take it that's a yes. Come on, sweetheart. Try to breathe slowly."

"Hurts." She would've cursed more, but that would've just added to the pain. She rested her head against Josiah's shoulder until it passed. Then she looked up and met his eyes. "I want to go home."

It was a totally irrational thing to say, but he nodded. "Let's get you up."

The inside of her jeans was stuck to her legs, but the discomfort of the clammy wetness barely registered. The fact that her bladder was about to burst annoyed her more. "I need a pit stop before you load me onto the bench seat."

"Need a hand?"

She waved him off. "This part I can do. Especially since I am not using the outhouse but peeing beside the house as if I were any of my redneck cousins."

"I'll get the truck started then come and get you," Josiah promised.

It didn't take her long. She wiggled out of her wet pants, intending to wrap herself up in the blanket she knew was in the truck. She made her way back, the noticeable lack of engine noises drawing her attention to Josiah who was shoving open the hood of the vehicle.

Oh, damn. "What's wrong?"

She would have offered to help, but this was one area where she had zero expertise. And when he stepped back and grimaced, she remembered he wasn't so hot with vehicles either. "Give me a minute."

He pulled out his phone.

She pulled out hers with pretty much zero expectation that they would have any kind of reception in this point of the mountains.

Yup. Zero bars.

Josiah met her gaze only seconds later. "Let's get you settled in the cabin, then I can go to Brad's for help."

Another contraction hit before they were even two steps away from the truck.

"Dammit." He would've picked her up and carried her, but she motioned him off. "Just let me stand here for a minute."

She'd been there while Tamara went through labour. The next time she saw her sister, Lisa would either be handing the woman a trophy or a fist in the face, because Tamara had made the pain seem tolerable.

Lisa was convinced she was being ripped in two.

From top to bottom, her skin had gone clammy, and stars danced in front of her eyes. But through it all, Josiah held her, talking quietly and soothing her.

If she had a baseball bat, she would've hit him with it right then. Really, really hard.

"I love you," she forced out between clenched teeth. "But I'm going to fucking kill you."

Josiah's lips twitched, but he followed her lead when she took a staggering step toward the cabin. "Hold that thought. Inside first."

The inside of the cabin held a table and chairs, a small kitchen area, and a woodburning fireplace. More than that, there was a queen-size bed tucked against one wall, and Lisa absolutely hated that they were about to make a mess of the cozy hideaway. "We're going to have the baby here, aren't we?"

"Maybe? Probably?" Josiah twisted until he could see her face. His confidence was back. "We're going to be okay. The *baby's* going to be okay. Only we need to talk about what we want to do."

I want to go home.

The words echoed in her head, but she managed to keep them from escaping her lips. "I think I'm in labour for real. We need to time my contractions."

"Do you want me to run to Brad's for help? It should take me about an hour and a half and then however long it takes for a crew to get up here on the return trip." He guided her to one of the straight-backed chairs at the table, and she settled into it gingerly, hand under the base of her belly where the contractions were the strongest.

She thought about it. Really thought about it. "Do you think we should?"

Josiah took a careful breath. "I think you are in prime physical condition, with no outstanding medical concerns. I think we can do this on our own, safely. But I can't guarantee it. So I will do whatever you need me to."

Her throat tightened slightly, which was not a good thing, considering she needed every bit of oxygen available so she could keep breathing, keep dealing with the contractions. "This is karma getting even for me calling you to be backup when Tamara went into labour, isn't it?"

A burst of laughter escaped him. "Well, that turned out okay in the end. So maybe it's karma's way of telling us that you can do it."

Another contraction wrapped itself around her. It squeezed her tight and pulled a shriek from her lips.

"Come on, sugar. Breathe. *Breathe.*"

Somehow Josiah wrapped his arms around her, his lips against her temple. He took a deep breath and let it out slowly, the sound like a steady rush of wind. It gave her something to imitate. To take a fraction of a second longer before she sucked in. She kept a death grip on his wrist until her muscles slowly unclenched once more.

"It's probably the smartest thing for you to go, but I don't want you to leave me," she confessed. Her mouth was dry, and her legs quivered, but for the moment, she could breathe and think straight.

She looked right into his eyes. "No matter what happens, this is the right choice. Stay with me. We'll do it together."

He dipped his chin decisively. Kissed her forehead then shot away. "I want to grab some things. Talk to me. The instant you feel the contraction start, I'll be there, and we'll get through this."

Which is how they spent their evening. The contractions were powerful from the beginning but far enough apart that Josiah managed to find everything he needed in the little cabin. He tried to restart the truck a number of times, but it was no use.

Besides, once Lisa knew that this was where they were staying, it made it easier for her to do a mental reset. She walked in circles around the tiny space. She picked some intriguing-looking objects to focus on when the contractions hit.

They even went out on the deck and into the field for a while as the sun headed toward the horizon and the entire sky went brilliant with orange and gold.

They had water, and they had food and clothing out of the emergency bin Brad kept stocked. He'd shown it to Josiah many moons ago because the cabin was used as an emergency stop during stormy weather.

Lisa was still alert enough to tease Josiah about the beautiful weather outdoors. "I'm so glad we're not stuck somewhere on the side of the highway in the middle of a snowstorm."

"On a scale of one to ten, a truck on the side of the highway in a snowstorm is a one. This ranks way the hell higher."

"I miss having a shower," she complained. "I was really looking forward to me and a hot shower."

Josiah was a lovely, sweet, *darling* man she decided she wouldn't kill after all, because the next thing she knew he had a bowl of water he'd warmed on the wood-fire stove, and a cloth. He washed the sweat off her face and wiped her limbs until she felt mostly human.

The contractions eventually began to speed up. She'd refused to make a mess in the bed, so instead they'd made a comfortable nest in the middle of the floor using pillows.

And then the contractions were one on top of the other, and it didn't matter what position she was in, it hurt, and then it hurt on top of the parts that already hurt. "I'm done," she told him. "I just want to sleep."

"Just a little bit more. We're nearly there." Josiah cupped her cheek again—such a sweet, tender action. Only she noticed he moved his hand away fast enough that if she did decide to bite him, she wouldn't have a chance to really grab on tight.

The sun was just beginning to rise, the darkness in the corners of the room being erased by more than candlelight and the golden glow from the glass in the air tight stove.

Ollie barked once, loudly.

The noise was a sudden shock after the peaceful quiet that had filled the cabin for so long. Peaceful, that is, except for her moaning and groaning—and the occasional curse.

Suddenly, the pain changed. Instead of being ripped apart, limb from limb, there was pressure building inside her that wanted to explode. "Josiah?"

He must've sensed her question because he was there, checking her before meeting her gaze with an excited nod. "It's time. You can push. Hold on tight."

When she told her sisters about it later, this was the part that she'd skip over because it was hazy, and very thankfully forgettable. Whatever magical hormones shot through her brain, it had to be something that helped people forget the traumatic moments of childbirth so they'd be willing to do it more than once.

But the other part of the magic was Josiah. Watching as his expression, already so filled with love, somehow grew brighter as their little girl arrived. There was the mess of the placenta to deal with, and there was crying, from both the baby and Lisa, but parts of it were beautiful, and the baby was perfect, and sunrise filled the room with so much promise.

However long after, Lisa held their baby girl against her naked torso. Josiah sat behind her, cradling them both as he murmured words of love. The baby had been cleaned and washed. Lisa had sipped water and had something to eat, and now they were wrapped up in a blanket, cuddling together as they savoured these first moments as a family.

"Does she look like a Zoë to you?" Lisa asked, stroking a finger against one perfect little cheek.

"She looks exactly like a Zoë," Josiah said. "Only, can I change her middle name?"

Lisa glanced up. He was staring at Zoë with absolute awe. "What do you want it to be?"

He pointed to the window and then to where they sat, painted by the golden light of morning. "Dawn? Sunshine? She's our little miracle, and I'm going to think of this moment every time I see her."

"Zoë Dawn Ryder." Lisa looked her over then nodded decisively. "I like it. I like it a lot." She tilted her head back so Josiah could see her face. "Hey, Daddy. I bet your sweetie name for her will be Sunshine."

"I bet you're right, Mommy." Josiah kissed her, then he kissed

Zoë, then he laughed because Ollie was there, tail wagging frantically as she asked to be let into the pile.

Josiah lifted the pup to a safe spot, close but not too close to the baby.

Ollie sniffed carefully before wiggling back. She settled at their feet, turning in a circle three times before lying down. She rested her nose on her paws as she breathed out a contented sigh as if she'd successfully completed the hugest and most important puppy task of all time.

Lisa leaned back on Josiah's chest and listened as his heartbeat wrapped around the three of them—the *four* of them—enveloping them with love.

*Bark, bark, bark***
*Ollie says *She knew first!*

I hope you enjoyed all these stories, especially the brand-new glimpse into Lisa and Josiah's growing family.

The coming year is going to bring more adventures to Heart Falls, so be sure that you've read the entire series and sign up for my newsletter so you don't miss any announcements.

NEXT... an excerpt from ROCKY MOUNTAIN FOREVER

PART V

ROCKY MOUNTAIN FOREVER EXCERPT

It's never too late for love.

Years ago, Mark Coleman made the only possible choice and left Rocky Mountain House before he tore his family apart. When he hears the four clans—Six Pack, Whiskey Creek, Moonshine and Angel—are working together to create a memory book, Mark also discovers the one detail that finally triggers his return.

Because he's not just coming back to the family. Now that Dana is free *and* ready to move on, Mark plans to give the only woman he's ever loved all the devotion and happiness she deserves, no matter how much sweet-talking, or dirty talk, it takes.

Meanwhile, when a shocking truth is shared with the oldest of the Six Pack sons, Blake Coleman begins a journey of assessment. Can he really fill his father's boots and be the leader his generation turns to for guidance?

With lots of visits with all your favourite Colemans, this is a celebration of love and the lessons learned along the way.

Warning: this book is full of happily-ever-afters. Lots of I love yous, lots of babies, lots of laughter and happy tears. Pretty much, readers familiar with the series have a ton of feel-good hours of reading ahead. If you want angst—this isn't it.

SP RANCH JOURNAL

~MICHAEL COLEMAN, FIRST JOURNAL ENTRY,
ONE WEEK AFTER THE PASSING OF HIS FATHER,
ROYCE COLEMAN, JANUARY 1983~

Life changed in a moment.

This was not what I expected--it's not the place I want to be. Yet, here we are. Suddenly I'm in charge of all of the Coleman holdings, and the privilege of it and the responsibility make my fingers tremble as I write this.

You made it look so simple, Da. Never a thing you couldn't do, and now you're gone, and hell if I know how to fill your boots.

Why didn't you say something—

No. I know exactly why you didn't say mention feeling sick. You were always strong. Always the first one up and caring for the family, making the tough decisions and working until you dropped. You didn't want us to know because you didn't want to admit to yourself that you weren't strong enough to fight sorrow and death. Damn stubborn fool.

It was clear you'd been a little lost the last couple of years, ever since Mom died. That wasn't a fault, you know. Caring so much that it broke your heart once she was gone. You taught us a lot with how much you loved.

I'm so glad I had you as a father, but sure as hell wish I'd been watching closer to see exactly how you made it look so easy. I'm not ashamed to admit I'm going to miss you even as I move forward, one foot after another. No use trying to solve problems that haven't even shown their faces yet.

Thank God for Marion, though, or I'd be in one hell of a mess. She's the one who got us through the funeral and the rest of it. Even hauling baby Matthew around with her, nothing slowed her down. Blake stuck by my side most of the time, the little tyke wide-eyed with his lip quivering, because even at not yet three, he knows his Grampa is gone.

And now I don't even know who I'm writing this for. You, the family...my sons?

Yet I know you journaled all the time. Somehow it feels right to pick up this part of your legacy. Can the act of copying something you did push me in the right direction?

Maybe it's wishful thinking to hope that, in putting pen to paper, I'll be able to work through troubled times. Maybe it'll let me savour the good times better.

Or perhaps somewhere between the two extremes of grief and joy, I can build a world that makes the Colemans rich. Not as in money overflowing from our pockets, but a family that's rock-solid far into the future. That's my goal.

Always did have more gusto than brains, but we'll see.

CHAPTER 1

December, present day, Six Pack ranch, Alberta

Darkness filtered to the edges of the room, the cool of the early December morning leaving the air outside the quilt crisp.

But the warmth in his arms told Blake Coleman everything he needed to know. Jaxi lay curled against him, face pressed to his chest, legs tangled with his. Skin on skin, the sweet scent of her filled his head and made his heart swell.

How he had this miracle in his life day after day—no idea. No damn idea what he'd done to deserve the goodness in his world.

She moved, head tilting back as her blue eyes opened the narrowest bit. Sleepy warmth and contentment all but dripped from her expression.

"Morning," she whispered.

Blake pressed his lips to hers, a smile curling his lips. "You're not rocketing out of bed like your panties are on fire."

She hummed, a secretive hush. "You're the one with the lighter. If there's going to be any panty bonfires—"

"Mama? Daddy?"

They both went silent.

It was a long shot. The chance to lay in bed late, neither of them needing to rush away for chores, was rare in the first place. Add in five kids, and Blake could count on one hand the number of mornings they'd had the room to themselves past five a.m. the past month.

When the quiet persisted, Blake began to relax.

Curled up against him, Jaxi pressed her lips against the side of his neck, easing her legs on either side of his. A throaty moan escaped her, and Blake wanted to both laugh and curse as he realized his hand no longer rested innocently on her hip. Nope. He'd full on cupped her ass and was even now in the process of dragging her on top of his body.

"Looking for trouble—" Jaxi began.

"*Maaaaama.*" The doorknob rattled as PJ's voice rang against the door. "*Daaaaaadeeeee.*"

Absolutely adorable even as their four-year-old's timing made Blake groan. "Invasion?" he asked Jaxi.

She pressed a quick kiss to his lips before carefully crawling off. "I'll get him. You deal with—*things.*"

With a slightly wicked pat of her hand against his belly, Jaxi swung away before he could grab her, hips wiggling saucily as she headed toward the door.

Blake rolled, adjusting his hard-on to a more comfortable position that was slightly protected in case their oldest son decided to jet propel his way onto the mattress like he usually did.

"Yes? We didn't order any pizza," Jaxi said as she knelt beside the door.

Around her, PJ's expression went utterly serious as he shook his head. "Not peeza. Cuddles."

"Well, that's totally different." Jaxi scooped him up, closing the door and returning to the bed. "Look, Daddy, we have an early morning delivery of cuddles."

"One of my favourite things," Blake said sincerely, opening his arms.

PJ snuggled in, and Blake felt that pulse deep inside again. The one that made him ache even as it brought a smile to his face.

Jaxi sat on the edge of the bed, her expression filled with wonder. "I love you."

She said the words so simply, but it was clear the message was meant for him, not their son. Although she totally loved their kids to pieces, this thing between *them* wasn't getting any smaller. After eight years of marriage it seemed to simply grow, expanding to fill every single bit of room, not just in Blake's heart, but in their home.

Even as he draped an arm around their son, he patted the mattress beside him. "Climb in. It's cold out there."

She smiled wryly. "I will. But I figured I'd wait to let the rest of them in first."

"Who—?"

He shouldn't have bothered asking. He knew the answer.

"Daddy?" A chorus of little girls.

Jaxi blew him a kiss before sneaking from the room. By the time she got back with two-year-old Justin in her arms, the seven-year-old blonde-haired twins, Rebecca and Rachel, had settled on either side of six-year-old Lana.

Lana sighed contentedly. "I like sleepovers."

"Not a sleepover when it's Mommy and Daddy's bed..." Becca explained seriously.

"...it's family cuddles," Rae finished.

"Shove over there, kids," Jaxi said with amusement. "Make room for your brother."

Shockingly, ten minutes later the bed was silent. The girls

had curled up in a heap like puppies and fallen back asleep almost immediately. Against Blake's chest, PJ's blondish hair spread in a tangled mess. He'd snuck his thumb in his mouth, his little chest moving easily.

Justin was sprawled on top of Jaxi, contented baby snores rising from him.

And Blake and Jaxi, teetering on the opposite edges of the mattress.

She was smiling, though. "Are you sure you don't want a king-size bed?"

Blake kept his chuckle soft to keep from waking anyone. "We had any more room in here, we'd be able to fit a couple of the dogs and a small horse."

She snapped a finger to her lips. "*Shh*. Do not suggest that, or the twins will try to sneak them in for a test run."

"The dogs? Or the horse?"

"Both. Either. *All* of them," Jaxi said, lips curling with amusement. Her gaze drifted over the family between them then back to Blake's eyes. "You need to take an extra-long lunch break."

He was lost for a moment before comprehension drifted in. While adult entertainment was out of the question this morning, it appeared there might be hope for later. "If you can find a bit of spare time in your day."

Her gaze grew heated. "Ashley and I are doing baby swaps this week. And it doesn't need to be a *bit*. Unless a *bit* means a couple of hours."

Reaching across the mass of children between them meant risking waking one or two. Blake satisfied himself with his best attempt at a smolder. "I'll be home by noon. We'll see what we can cook up together."

The delight on his woman's face was as sweet as the family that lay between them and as heated as the plans that lay before them.

They stared at each other in silence, smiles on their faces, love pooling around them for another hour until it was time to head into the day.

The chaos of breakfast followed. Then backpacks and getting three little girls off to the school bus, all of them bundled up in their snow suits.

Jaxi kissed him sweetly before grabbing PJ's hand. Justin peeked out of the backpack contraction she wore. "We're headed over to the Peter's house. I promised I'd watch the kids this morning so Ashley can do some painting."

Blake shook his head in amazement. Ashley, Cassidy and Travis already had three kids, the youngest born only three months ago. "Five kids under the age of four. You're a glutton for punishment."

"She'll have them this afternoon, starting at lunch," Jaxi reminded him, eyes brightening. "Besides. It's nice to hold a teeny baby again."

Her idea of a good time was far too exhausting for him. "See you at noon," he promised.

They were well enough set up these days at the Six Pack ranch. By sharing land and sharing responsibilities between all the Coleman clans, the sense of urgency they'd all faced years before had lessened. The struggle to provide for all the family had been dealt with. While there were still moments of uncertainty, because nothing about ranching could be predicted to go smoothly, having the holdings back together had begun to create some wonderful opportunities.

Everyone's expertise got used where they were most valuable. It meant no longer juggling to find enough grazing land or seed land or feed.

Although he did miss having his cousin Karen from the Whiskey Creek side of the family around, with the way she had with horses. She and her sisters had settled about a three-hour drive to the south of Rocky, which always struck Blake as odd.

He couldn't think of *any* reason why family would want to leave. Still, she seemed happy enough. Maybe when she came to visit this weekend for their early Christmas gathering, he could bend her ear for a while. Get some ideas of where she thought the Colemans should go with their horse breeding plans.

He'd barely finished his morning paperwork when Jesse stuck his head in the door of the office. "This is where you're hiding."

Blake pushed the chair in then joined his brothers in the main barn. He nodded at Travis before turning back to Jesse. "Wasn't hiding, but getting up to date. Looks as if *you* need to hit the books for a bit. Took a peek at your project, and doesn't look as if you're done."

Jesse shook his head. "One more push should do it. The last time I tried to finish up, we had that power outage, and I lost about three hours of data entry."

The genetics program Jesse was using to help amalgamate the Coleman ranch more fully was state-of-the-art, but old wiring in creaky barns was hell on modern technology. "Shit. Didn't know that."

Jesse shrugged. "Pain in the ass, but it happens. Sorry I'm a little slow. If you need the information right away, I can stay late tonight. I don't mind if it takes longer to get it done."

Well.

Blake eyed him sideways. That was just so not Jesse that both Blake and Travis caught it.

His little brother was no longer a lazy butt, or the type to try to wiggle out of work. He also had a wife he was head over heels about, and a kid he adored, *plus* his twin brother and family living right next door. Jesse and Joel were as tight as anything once again.

Jesse deliberately volunteering to be late getting home?
Nope.

Travis obviously had gone through the same thought process. He raised a brow. "Dare kick you out?"

"No," Jesse snapped, but then he looked just about as guilty as Rae had the day before when she'd been caught with her fingers in the cookie jar right before supper. "Not really. Sort of."

"Ha." Travis was grinning way too hard. "And if you want to work late, that means you're also in shit with Joel, because otherwise you'd go hang out with him until Dare wants to see your ugly mug again."

A heavy sigh escaped Jesse. "They're *all* pissed at me."

Joel, his wife Vicki, and Dare? "That's quite the accomplishment." Somehow Blake kept his expression from twisting into a smile. "You deserve it?"

"Probably." Jesse flashed a grin. "It'll be okay. I'll let Dare cuss me out a few times, and then I'll work all the kinks out between us with some makeup sex."

"You can get out of the doghouse that fast?" Travis shook his head. "You need to fight a little harder. I mean, makeup sex is good and all, but they need to be really lit on fire for it to be extra fun."

"The man who has two spouses to get mad at him at the same time thinks fighting is fun?" Blake shook his head. "There's a name for people like you."

Travis actually sputtered for a second before grinning broadly.

Jesse rolled his eyes dramatically then confessed the truth.

"Because *that* conversation is going places I don't want to talk about, it was just a misunderstanding. And yeah, Dare was right —I stuck my nose in where it didn't belong." Jesse leaned back on the wall behind him, folding his arms over his chest. "I walked in on Vicki and Joel having what I thought was a full out, drag-down fight. I waded into the middle because I knew they'd be upset if they actually tossed bullshit at each other that hard. But it turns out they were reciting some damn movie, and Dare was there, and so all three of them gave me hell."

Travis snorted. "A *movie*? For fucks sake, can't you guys even fight about something that's not comical?"

"Screw you, asshole."

"Diva."

"Loser."

"Jerk."

"Ahhh, brotherly love." Blake slapped a hand at the side of Travis's head, dodging out of the way before his brother's instant roundhouse could connect. "Stop your jawing and let's get to work."

The entire morning was filled with goodness of hard, honest labour, followed by a sweet, dirty interlude that left Blake grinning for most of the afternoon.

He thought about all the blessings in his world and wondered—

A sense of foreboding hung over him. Like everything was *too* good to be true. Something was going to rush in and shake things up in a way he couldn't anticipate.

Totally superstitious nonsense, but it felt so real. He paused before leaving the barn to head back to Jaxi and his family, pausing to rap his knuckles against the sturdy wooden frame of the man door for luck.

What they had was priceless—was precious. He didn't want anything to change.

CHAPTER 2

The time it took to drive to his home in the middle of the Six Pack land wasn't long enough to give Jesse a solution to his problem.

The concern, he could honestly admit, wasn't the fact the three people he cared most about in the world had been mad at him before he left the house that morning. Travis had been right —it was a stupid thing to fight about, and Dare had been justified in calling him on sticking his nose in where it wasn't needed. That misdeed had probably been forgiven before his truck had even left the driveway.

Nope, if there was one thing he was absolutely certain about —Dare loved him unconditionally, even when he was an ignorant bastard. And both Joel and Vicki cared enough to call him on his bullshit.

It was like being wrapped in a warm blanket on this icy cold December day to have that kind of gut-deep assurance in his world.

His problem—

Jesse stuck his hand in the pocket of his sheepskin-lined jacket and worried the envelope another time. Half a dozen times that day he'd considered pulling it out of his pocket and showing it to Blake, but he knew better. Even as tangled as the out of the blue offer made his brain, it was Dare he needed to talk to first.

And obviously, ignoring the proposal he'd received wasn't the way to go. He thought he could put it off until the new year, but the information kept buzzing at the back of his brain. Distracting him and screwing with his concentration.

Hell. Jesse knew better than to get between his brother and his wife, for more reasons than most.

What was worse, there was no reason to sit there suffering. No reason why he *wasn't* telling Dare exactly what was bothering him.

The final approach up the road to Sunset Ridge added to both the deep sense of contentment and the concern dredging through every part of his body.

Nearly identical houses sat silhouetted against the skyline, showcasing the comfortable yet compact homes where he and his twin were raising their families. It was everything he'd ever dreamed of—to be living next to his best friend, head over heels in love with a wonderful woman who was more than his equal. A beautiful little boy.

The excitement of discovering their family would be growing—Dare was expecting in July.

Jesse's fingers tightened instinctively around the envelope, and he cursed. The urge to throw the letter away, or burn it, was so damn strong. Yet, he couldn't.

He pulled into the parking space next to Joel's truck, a grin coming unbidden as he glanced over to find his brother sitting behind the wheel waiting for him.

They both got out, meeting at the shoveled walkway that led toward the houses.

Joel eyed him with amusement. "Well, that's disappointing."

Confusion hit. "What?"

"I asked Blake to make you shovel shit all day. Doesn't look like I got my wish."

Jesse used his middle finger to scratch the bridge of his nose. "Hope you had fun on lost sheep duty. Find them all, Bo Peep?"

"Ass." Only Joel was grinning. "Cassidy and Matt called in the Moonshine clan. We got the entire herd back into the lower pasture, plus all the fences fixed and gates shut. The rest of the season is going to be a piece of cake."

That was good news. "I really like this working with the entire family business," Jesse shared honestly.

"It's damn handy," Joel agreed. "Although it's going to take a couple of years to get all the cows onto the same season. I'm not looking forward to them dropping all the way from February till May."

"One thing at a time," Jesse said. It was one of the things he was working on with his programming. He met his brother's gaze straight on. "I said it this morning, but I'll say it again. I'm sorry. I butt in where it wasn't my right. I'm glad you told me to fuck off."

Joel nodded once. "Vicki and I were more pissed that you thought we would say such crappy things to each other."

"That's the part that threw me," Jesse insisted. "You and Vicki—if anything, you're way too sweet and gushy. You don't toss words like knives."

"Good to know we've got you fooled." His brother shrugged. "Don't kid yourself. We still screw up, and words get heated. But we don't let it stick. I swear Vicki's been taking lessons from Mom—"

A laugh escaped before Jesse could stop it. "Jeez, you too?"

Joel dipped his chin "The last time I was ticked off about something, she plopped down on the footstool by my chair and waited."

"Which means you have to talk about it. Or you have to admit 'I'm pissed off and don't want to talk to you right now' which is okay some of the time, but mostly sounds as if I'm about eight years old and pitching a fit."

They both chuckled before Joel let out a long slow sigh. "This is probably why Mom and Dad's fights are virtually nonexistent."

"Because he knows he can't win?" Jesse teased.

"Can we?"

"More importantly, do we want to?" Jesse winked before turning toward the path that led to his house. "We're on shift together tomorrow?"

"Six a.m. You drive. Vicki needs the truck to pick up supplies for the Christmas party this weekend."

Another thing Jesse had forgotten about in his distracted haze. "It'll be good to see the Whiskey Creek girls again."

After a final solid thump on the shoulder, Joel turned away and headed whistling toward his home.

Jesse did the same.

Inside, golden light shone onto the wintry landscape and reflected off the walls to fill the cozy space. Both the heat and the scent of dinner welcomed him in.

"*Daddy.*" Enough noise for a platoon of kids rushed toward him. His son, wearing a teeny pair of cowboy boots and riding a stick horse across the hardwood floor.

"Hey, Buckaroo." Jesse swooped down and nabbed Joey, horse and all. "Where's your mama?"

"'puter."

"Ah. She's still working?"

"She's done." Dare rounded the corner, and here was the true welcome. She squeezed up against him, Joey cradled between them. "Hey. I didn't expect you for another half hour."

"Blake sent me home. Told me I needed to come apologize before you decided I had to sleep in the barn."

"Horsies," Joey exclaimed.

"Yes. The horses live in the barn. Daddy lives with *us*, even when he's being—" Dare paused.

"Go on," Jesse encouraged. "I not only want to hear what you say, but I want to know how you're going to say it in a buckaroo-approved matter."

Her eyes flashed, but he thought it was with amusement. "—even when he's being a buttinski."

Joey's little face curled up in a frown. "Daddy buttski?"

Laughter escaped.

"Yes," Dare agreed, squeezing Jesse and lifting her lips for a kiss.

"Don't blame me when that kid says things we'd rather he didn't in front of Grandma," Jesse warned with a whisper in her ear.

"We'll blame Grandpa."

Worked for him. Jesse pulled her tight. "Hello, love. I missed you today."

Then he kissed her. A sweet moment that made being apart bearable because he knew this was the reward waiting. The coming back together was not just fire and heat—although they had plenty of that between them.

After nearly three years the *quiet* moments were growing richer. The conversations and the searching for the next adventure to share were being built on a firm foundation.

Jesse was damn grateful.

Her lips on his, the heat of her body and the swells of her breasts pressed against him were also something to be thankful for. Joey squirmed, and Jesse put the boy back on the ground.

Catching Dare's hand, he held her in place when she would've taken off to the kitchen. "I apologized to Joel, and now it's your turn. I was out of line this morning. Thanks for giving me hell. I was distracted, but that's not an excuse."

Dare lowered her chin slowly. "Okay."

Then she waited.

For one moment Jesse wanted to burst into laughter, because it was exactly what he and Joel had just talked about. "You're not going to let me leave it at that, are you?"

She winked then headed toward the back of the house. "Of course, I am. For now. Go. Grab a shower, and I'll finish supper. I can wait until later to poke you to find out what's wrong."

It wasn't until Joey was fast asleep in bed that Jesse brought it up. Taking Dare by the hand, he led her into the living room and in front of the fire he'd lit in the airtight stove.

Dare sat beside him, arms wrapped around her legs. "This looks serious."

"I guess it is." All evening his admission to Joel had been echoing in his head. The part about how much he enjoyed working with his family. With all of the Coleman clan. Jesse pulled the letter out of his pocket, running his hand over it in a futile effort to straighten some of the wrinkles before passing it over. "I got this in the mail a couple of days ago."

She examined the envelope. "University of Alberta." A small furrow formed between her brows. "There a problem with your school records—*wait*. You went to Old's College, not the University."

Jesse pointed at the letter. "One of my profs moved. It's all kind of technical, but I guess the program he taught us to use was experimental. Somebody with a bunch of money wanted to invest in agricultural technology, and I was one of the guinea pigs."

She nodded. "Go on."

This was the part where it got a little unreal. "One of the things Dr. Wadia asked was for any students who used the program to send him periodic updates. For data analysis—that kind of thing."

"I remember that. I remember you asked my brother for permission to share after you did some programming for them down at Silver Stone." Dare no longer looked worried but very curious. "Caleb said both he and Luke really appreciated your help."

"They weren't the only ones." Jesse took a deep breath. "There's more, but long story short—Dr. Wadia's got a research grant that starts in September next year. They're going to run a five-year program, including regular travel to other countries to help them set up their own systems."

Dare went very still. "He didn't write just to tell you his exciting news, did he?"

Jesse shook his head. "He wants me to join him. He wants me to be one of the main programmers on the project, including teaching and travelling."

Dare sat back, sprawled on her arms she gazed at him with on her eyes. "Jesse. That's a huge complement. It's amazing."

It was—and the mere thought of it tangled his insides into a thousand knots. "I don't know what to do."

She was too far away. Jesse pulled Dare into his lap. He circled her with his arms and buried his face against her neck. Her rich auburn hair fell around him like a curtain, blocking out everything except the two of them. The warmth of her body melded against his, the heated brush of her breath ghosted past his ear.

"We'd have to move away from your family, and farther from mine." Dare's words were barely a whisper. "Away from Vicki and Joel."

"Away from all of them, yes." Jesse took a deep breath and straightened slightly, cupping her cheek. "My first instinct is to say no, but there's a hefty salary involved. And I do mean *hefty*—

the corporation that's funding the research has deep pockets. We need to think seriously about this."

"When do you have to decide by?"

"There's no rush," Jesse said. "Dr. Wadia says he's getting the first steps of the process in place, but wanted to give me a heads up. He should know it's a go for sure by the end of April. The absolute deadline for my decision is August first."

"Wow."

Silence reigned again for a while before Dare nodded decisively. "Well, I can see why you were distracted. But the fact that we've got a long time to make a decision means we need to not worry right now. Especially if he won't know until the end of April if he actually has a job to offer you."

It was good advice, but Jesse knew he would still think about it a lot more than was good for him.

He went for a topic change. "You're not mad at me anymore?"

"Nothing to be mad about," she insisted.

"I'm a little pissed that you're being so understanding," Jesse confessed. "I could use a little arguing."

Dare rolled her eyes. "Yeah, because throwing dishes and shouting is so much more fun."

He rolled her to the carpet, pinning her under his body. "It's not the shouting that's fun, it's what comes after."

"Oh, *that's* the part you're missing." Her gaze shifted to his lips. "We can probably come up with a reason why we need to have some angry sex. It is angry sex that you looking for?"

"Angry. Hot. Heavy." He jammed a hand under her shirt and slid it upward until her breast filled his palm. "I want to take you hard."

Instead of telling him he was an ass or yawning in his face, both responses he would've completely understood, Dare proved once again she was his absolutely perfect partner.

She grinned. "I think we can manage that."

Unexpectedly, she twisted. With a hand on his shoulder, she got enough torque to flip into his back. An instant later, she'd crawled over him, peeling her shirt up and over her head to toss it aside.

Jesse hummed in approval. He curled up far enough to undo her bra and sent it flying after her shirt. "Your tits are always stunning, but pregnant? There should be an entire wing in some museum to pay homage to them."

"They're big enough to fill an entire wing by themselves," Dare teased before moaning. "God, Jesse. *Yes.*"

He didn't know what to do next. He wanted it all. His hands, his mouth, his teeth all over her skin. He dropped his hands to her waistline, rolling her under him as he shred away her pants and undies.

Dare stripped his shirt away, fabric tore. They were all hands and heat and dirty delicious noises—far too long, yet it was only moments later he dipped his fingers between her legs and found her ready and wet for him.

"Do it." Dare made the words a challenge, a gasp following as he hauled her over his legs and notched himself against her heat.

One inch. One thrust and they were joined.

Their foreheads met. "You are my everything," Jesse confessed.

Her face lit up like sunshine. "Good. Now fuck me."

With pleasure. For both of them.

He rocked into her hard and dirty, soaking in the sensations streaking over his skin like wild fire. Aching with the extreme pleasure of the tight fist of her body surrounding him. Dare's heels dug into his ass as she rocked to meet his demands with her own vibrant enthusiasm.

He paused for a moment to lick his thumb then reached between their bodies to slide over her clit.

Dare arched, her breasts pressing against his naked chest. Head falling back, her hair slid over his arm supporting her back. Sweaty and hot with every bit of pleasure centered in his core as she squeezed him, taking as hard as he gave.

A moment later her nails raked across his shoulders and she let out a cry. He lost it, the connection between them fire and passion.

They clung to each other, chests heaving. Coming down while still connected. Bodies, souls. Hearts.

Dare sighed happily. "I love you. We'll figure it out."

"I love you, too," he agreed. "And we will."

Jesse just hoped the right answer wouldn't require tearing his heart in two.

SP RANCH JOURNAL
~MICHAEL COLEMAN, JANUARY 1984~

*S*till *trying to figure out where the hell the past twelve months flew to.*

With the successful year we've had, it's time. I know Da intended to someday divide the land into six sections, one for each of us boys to be able to take charge of and find our way.

I'm in total agreement. Just because I had to take over when I did doesn't mean I'm the best man for all the tasks. Plus, I know our hearts lie in different areas. If I have to listen to George wax poetically about his damn horses for another three straight hours…

He's got interesting plans, and I bet they work, but as far as I'm concerned, a horse is part of the working ranch and not a pretty work of art to be pranced around an arena.

Like I said—different paths, neither right nor wrong.

It's clear though, that John's never going to fully take charge of his section. We'll deal with it easily enough, and he'll never want. He's a fantastic worker—when things are going well. I've done everything I can to get him to see a doctor, or a therapist, but he's stubborn. Like all us Colemans, so I guess I'm not surprised. But the land will be his, and when he's up to it, we chat about his ideas, but mostly, he hangs out with Mark and works beside his twin.

I've asked Mark if he's okay with that, and he insists he is. If it ever changes—

Well, I'm keeping an eye on it.

Three of us are married now—myself, Ben, and Randy. George and Sally got engaged over the holidays, and plan to get married the summer after next. Not sure why they're waiting so long on the wedding because George told me they already plan to move in together into the house he's working on as soon as it's done. Again— different paths.

I keep hoping Mark will find someone he's interested in. Even sent him to the Stampede and on as many buying and selling trips as I could wrangle in the hopes someone from outside Rocky would catch his eye, but so far, no luck.

His business is his own, but I've made sure he knows he's welcome to bring anyone home, no matter who he falls in love with. Colemans are smart enough to accept the person for who they are, not anything else.

In other news, Marion had an idea. Said we're all getting to the point that our individual families need to build some of their own traditions, even as we spend time together. Christmas Day is for families, Boxing Day for the entire Coleman clan. She has spoken—and I'm not about to argue, because she's right. As usual.

Still, we don't want to leave anyone out. Since they don't have extended families yet, Mark and John were invited over to Ben and Dana's for Christmas Day. For some reason, Mark ended up here instead. Said he promised Blake he'd take him tobogganing. No idea what's going on there. Maybe he and Ben had another fight—oil and water those two at times—but I didn't mind having my kid bro around. Marion just rolled her eyes, set another place at the table then made him wash the dishes.

The party on Boxing Day was just what we needed. Adults all caught up with each other, the four kids tangled happily like pigs in a pen.

I'm going to suggest we do it all over again later this year—maybe July 1st. While we get together often, putting those dates aside could make it extra special. Family gatherings are important. I can see them getting even more so as the Coleman clan continues to grow.

CHAPTER 3

Jaxi pulled the final batch of cookies from the pantry from where she'd stashed them and handed the container to her mother-in-law. "I think that's it for us at the main house. Ashley's got everything ready over at the Peter's house for the guys."

Marion glanced around the home that had once been where she raised her six boys. "You did the place up nice."

"Not much different than usual," Jaxi insisted. "Although the poinsettias you and Mike got us really brighten up the room. Thanks for that. Makes it look extra festive in here."

Marion picked her coffee off the table and gestured toward the easy chairs. "Come sit for a minute. Chaos will arrive soon enough."

Jaxi grabbed her own drink, happy to have a moment alone with the older woman. She paused to peek into the playpen to check if Justin was still covered up. "What are the chances he'll try and stay awake the entire time people are here?"

"They'll be enough hands that all the babies will get passed around just fine," Marion assured her. She took a sip of her coffee and smiled contentedly. "I kind of like that we're holding an extra holiday get-together for the Colemans this year." She glanced at Jaxi. "Of course, I can say that because *I'm* not the one who did all the extra organizing."

"It made sense. I've missed seeing the Whiskey Creek girls since they moved away. When they said they wouldn't be coming north for Boxing Day, it made sense to put it a little extra effort."

"Still, thank you. And I know your Uncle George is grateful. It's about time we got a chance to meet that new daughter of his."

Which seemed to Jaxi like one of those fairytale moments. "Poor girl. I can't imagine what it must feel like to walk into a family gathering this size."

"She's a Coleman by blood. She'll have the guts to handle it." Marion nodded firmly. "Besides, she'll have her sisters."

Which was true, yet Jaxi made a mental note to ask a couple of the quieter Coleman ladies to keep an eye on Julia when she arrived. It didn't matter how brave somebody was, getting tossed into a gathering of strangers you wanted to impress was never going to be a walk in the park.

Jaxi's oldest sister-in-law, Beth, could calm a raging storm. Partly it was her teacher training and partly the woman just oozed Zen-like vibes. Jaxi appreciated her for many reasons but was especially grateful one of their more immediate family members had no problem being the peacefulness to counter Jaxi's admittedly high-energy leanings.

She caught herself smiling. Her sister-in-law Ashley next door was possibly an equal match in enthusiasm and energy. Jaxi had never imagined back when Travis had first brought his partners home that his wife would be so much fun to be around.

Ashley was the master of everything crafty, with an artistic flair that left Jaxi in awe. Most recently the other woman had designed a snugly to swaddle her babies that could be done up with one hand—a miracle in any mother's books. Add in the blankets were sinfully soft and made of the brightest, happiest fabric their sister-in-law Hope could bring into her quilting store, and everyone in the community wanted one.

Sitting in the cozy living room, Jaxi gazed around at the comfortable home she'd made with Blake. The signs of children were everywhere, and while the furniture might be a little worn, it was still bright and pretty.

"It's a wonderful place." Marion said firmly.

Jaxi glanced up, amused. "Can you read my face that clearly?"

"Probably because I've seen that expression on my own face so many times," Marion returned. "We've had things good over-all, haven't we?"

"Better than good. Pretty much everything I've ever hoped for." Jaxi played with the cup in her hands. It was true, but there'd been one thing twisting inside her over the last while that she'd been wondering about hard.

After Justin had been born, she'd told Blake they were done having babies. It wasn't until Ashley's most recent had arrived in September that something had changed. Holding their newest nephew had woken up a part of Jaxi that she'd thought was ready to be done.

But that was a conversation to put aside until at least after the party this weekend.

It wasn't until the afternoon that the gathering officially started. The family met in the front yard of Blake and Jaxi's then broke into two. The men half scooped up the older kids and hauled them across the coulee to Ashley, Travis and Cassidy's place.

Blake came and gave Jaxi a final hug, a trio of little blonde girls and one four-year-old boy bouncing around his legs like jumping beans. He leaned in. "Have fun making mischief."

Jaxi pressed a hand to her chest. "Us? A choir of angels couldn't be more innocent."

Becca tugged on Jaxi's leg. "We're going tobogganing. Uncle Jesse said he once slid down the hill in the coulee and…"

"…went right over the river and up the other side." Rae finished.

Jaxi's gaze snapped to Blake's face. "Uncle Jesse sometimes has a problem remembering the rules."

"We're going to the *other* tobogganing hill," Blake informed the girls firmly before offering Jaxi a quick wink. "The one that Uncle Jesse doesn't know how to slide down nearly as good as you guys. You'll probably have to teach him."

"Uncle Jesse is silly," Lana pronounced with the wisdom of a six-year-old. "We'll teach him the right way."

"Wight way," PJ agreed.

"You do that," Jaxi encouraged.

Happiness bubbled in her chest as Blake gave her another quick kiss. "I promise they'll return with all body parts intact."

"You as well. I like all your body parts," she said with an utterly straight face. "*Ohh.*" She slapped a hand over the spot on her butt where he'd pinched her.

Then she hurried over to greet Ashley and take the car seat from her. "Ready to share your babies?"

Ashley grinned, twisting to the side to display one-year-old River peeking over the side of the backpack. He blinked huge dark eyes as he clutched strands of Ashley's hair as if they were reins on a pony. "Anyone who can get this kid to let go of me for more than thirty seconds is welcome to try."

Blonde-haired Daisy toddled over to Jaxi, her riotous curls poking out from underneath her knitted toque.

"Auntie J., up," she ordered, arms held out demandingly. With three adults in the house willing to offer hugs at the drop of a hat, the little sweetie was wee bit of a tyrant.

Jaxi got the two-year-old balanced on her hip then between her and Ashley, carried the car seat about five feet before Trevor and Becky from the Moonshine clan showed up.

"I've got him," Trevor insisted, pulling the car seat away and peeking inside. "Hey, dude. You want to come hang out with the big boys?"

"Sure, Trev. Just remember Forest will need to be burped and probably changed. After you nurse him, that is," Ashley teased.

Trevor made a face. "Too bad, little guy. Tell you what. This time you keep an eye on your mom and your cousin-to-be."

He stood, carrying the car seat in one hand and wrapping the other arm around Becky to stabilize her. "Come on, Rodeo. Let's get you inside where it's warm."

Becky smile was patient. "I'm plenty warm, Trevor. I have this internal heat system helping." She glanced at Jaxi. "I don't know how anybody stands being pregnant in the summertime."

Then they were in the house and coats were being pulled off. Trevor actually got Forest out of his car seat and was cradling the three-month-old with a far more experienced air than Jaxi had expected.

He grinned when he caught her staring. "With my little brother and his wife having Irish twins, the entire Moonshine clan has gotten a lot of practice lately holding babies."

Everyone moved into the living space, and once the dust settled, Becky cradled Forest, staring down at his dark hair with a secretive smile on her lips. Ashley still held River, and everywhere else Jaxi's sisters-in-law and the woman of the other Coleman clans were settling into chairs and beginning to catch up.

The Whiskey Creek Coleman girls entered the house to loud cheering. The newest member of the family, Julia, stood beside them, her cheerful grin shining out.

Lisa gestured toward their group. "I'm pleased to present the now complete Whiskeyteer four-pack. Everybody, this Julia. Julia," Lisa swung her hand as if she were a game show host, "this is everybody."

Julia wiggled her fingers. "I don't see any nametags."

"Just call us Ms. Coleman, and you'll be mostly right." Marion said dryly as laughter bloomed again.

The next hour passed in sweet pleasure as everyone visited for a while then rotated and moved to a new group of family. Babies were passed around with joy and love.

Rachel from the Moonshine clan sank back on the couch with a contented sigh as she breast-fed two-month-old Ava and watched her one-year-old, Liam, take toddling steps toward Lisa. "There's been something in the water, hasn't there?"

Jaxi glanced around the room. "We've been blessed, yeah."

Rachel snickered. "The Coleman family is funding Doctor Kincaid's retirement all by ourselves."

"He has delivered just about all of our babies, hasn't he?"

"Here's an opening if I ever heard one." Dare got to her feet. She grinned as she checked around the room, little Joey playing some game with stacking blocks with two of his cousins. "Becky here is on the calendar for a March baby. Melody and Anna are using June for a second round of 'can we have our babies on the same day and give them incredibly similar nicknames?'."

"I had Jay picked out for a long time," Melody insisted.

"Kay was born first. That's all I'm saying." Anna folded her arms over her chest. "You're just such a copycat."

Melody proved she was one hundred percent Coleman at this stage of the game. She stuck out her tongue at her sister-in-law.

"So far you're only telling us things we already know," Jaxi pointed out. "Unless you're ready to add to that list?"

Dare grinned. "We've booked a mid-July appointment. This time it wasn't an oops."

The laughter and congratulations had barely begun when Vicki stood, her smile brilliant. "Joel and I are excited to let you all know baby number two is on the way, also expecting mid-July."

Dare's draw dropped. "No way."

"Way." Vicki threw her arms around Dare and squeezed tight. "I'm so happy we get to do it together this time."

"Because synchronized vomiting is such a good thing to share." But her obvious excitement was clear. Dare pulled away and offered a wink. "I can't think of anyone I'd prefer to share that experience with."

"Awwww."

As the room quieted, Auntie Kate got to her feet and turned to the rest of the older generation. "I'm going to take a wander over to the other house," she announced. "Marion? Dana? Want to take a peek and see if the guys are holding it together?"

"We might need to stop in the office for a few minutes,' Marion said with a smile. "I know where Mike hides the good hootch."

"I'm all for that," Auntie Dana said. She pointed a finger at her daughter-in-law Laurel. "You're my designated driver, right?"

The blonde-haired woman grinned. "Because you're always such a party animal? Go on. Drink away."

Jaxi waited until the door was firmly closed behind her mother-in-law and aunts before turning to the group and rubbing her hands together. "Okay, ladies, put your thinking caps on. I've got an idea."

A chorus of groans mixed with a lot of snickering greeted her announcement.

"Why does it sound as if I should be worried?" Julia asked quietly from where she'd settled between Beth and Becky.

"Because you have good instincts. Jaxi's been itching to do something grandiose ever since last year with Marian and

Mike's fortieth anniversary." Beth glanced at Jaxi over the top of her teacup. "I don't think you've recovered from that disappointment yet."

Jaxi threw her hands in the air. "It's not fair. It would've been a perfect time to do something up, family-wise."

Beth turned to the newcomer in the room "Jaxi likes to organize things."

"This is true."

"Gospel truth."

"Not a word of lie in it."

The words echoed on the air without anyone taking credit for calling out the quick phrases.

Well, now.

Jaxi folded her arms over her chest then took the mature route. It was *her* turn to stick out her tongue at the gathered women.

Beth continued her explanation, amusement tingeing her voice. "Only Marion said that she wanted their fortieth to be about where they were now, not what had been, so all of Jaxi's plans to put together some kind of family history were dashed because—well, you just don't give somebody a present they don't want."

"That makes sense." Julia still looked a little wide-eyed, glancing around the room that was filled with Colemans and kids. "Also, wouldn't that have only been the Six Pack history? And there's four families, right?"

"Actually, there were six brothers. One passed away, four still live here in Rocky, plus Uncle Mark, who's sort of like my Guardian angel." This from Becky. She turned her gaze on Jaxi. "I'm on your side. If your idea is to make some sort of overall family record."

"Only, it's got to be something that the next generation will actually want. Straight up journals are boring." This from

Rachel who was cradling her now sleeping daughter. "Think about who will want this fifty years from now."

Dare was nodding slowly. She'd run a successful blog for years at this point, and Jaxi was curious what she'd suggest to make this idea even better. "Turn the spotlight on *any* event. It doesn't have to be only the big occasions like weddings or that kind of stuff. It's more important the events have solid *memories* attached. Happy, or sad, or something that changes you."

"So, you're saying we need...the feelings?" Laurel wrinkled her nose. "Pictures aren't enough?"

"I'm saying it's got to have context. Baby pictures are great *if* we know who they are so we can see who looks like who." Dare smiled. "For example, Marion gave me a picture of Jesse as a toddler making a terrible face. It's funny on its own, but it's even better when she told me that was the first time Jesse tried ice cream, and he *hated* it. He refused to try any again for years."

"Really?" Jaxi laughed. "I didn't know that."

Dare grinned. "Stories make it special."

Lisa chuckled, just loud enough to have all the heads in the room swinging in her direction. "This one is easy. Get the uncles into one room and pass around some pictures. Then record what they say. Trust me, you'll get the stories."

"You know what, that's *it*." Jaxi snapped up a finger at Lisa. "But not just the uncles, *all* of us. *Everybody's* memories—at least one from each family member—the good ones, the ones that are real, even the bad things."

"The ones that involve food, which means mostly good, *especially* if I'm involved." Vicki offered a wink as laughter rippled around the room. "Well, it's true."

"If you include recipes, I can guarantee the guys will crack the family history open," Dare said with a nod.

"A joint family memory book," Jaxi said. "With pictures, but more importantly, the stories, and the recipes, that go with them." She glanced around the room, excitement rising as a ton of ideas rushed into her head. "What do you guys think? We could take our time on it, but if everyone helped, we could put it together in digital format for us, and print for the older generation."

"Take our time?" Ashley grinned. "So, like, you want our essays of what we did over the holidays on your desk January fifth?"

"Of course not." Jaxi rolled her eyes dramatically before teasing back. "You can have until the beginning of February."

"Ha. How about you set up some guidelines, and we'll just keep going at it until we're done. *No* deadlines." Ashley winked. "It took a while to make the memories. We may as well enjoy stirring them up."

It was a good idea, because there were too many people to simply herd in the right direction quickly. Jaxi nodded. "This should be fun, not something we dread, so taking our time is important."

"And if we want everyone to share, we need to let them consider what they *want* to share. Especially the older stuff." Laurel was thinking hard. "There are all kinds of random old boxes in the attic at Angel ranch."

"At the Peter's place as well," Ashley agreed.

"I can help go through things. And I'll get Trevor to write to Uncle Mark and let him know what's going on." Becky smiled, her hands resting gently on her belly as she met Jaxi's gaze. "They keep in touch. I'm so glad."

The conversation drifted to holiday activities, and food, and between the laughter and the occasional burst of crying from the little ones, the house was full of life and happiness.

And a goal. Jaxi soaked in the sensation of family and considered the question herself.

Of her many memories, which was the most important?

Something about becoming a part of the Coleman family? About falling in love? It wasn't as if she could only contribute one thing, but she didn't want to miss the chance to share a truth that would become a part of the forever history of the clan.

This was going to take time, and she planned to enjoy every minute of it.

CHAPTER 4

Christmas card from Trevor Coleman to Uncle Mark

*onsidering I write to you about every two weeks, it sure
seems there's a lot to catch up on.*

*First off—you should admire the Christmas card.
Ashley (from the Six Pack side of things) made an entire set using
pictures the little kids in the clan drew. I think this one is supposed to
be the reindeer pulling Santa's sled, but my nephew Jay is only two
and a half and apparently any artistic talent he inherited will involve
music, not art. Or Jay thinks reindeer and elephants are related, in
which case, he drew them very well.*

*Another holiday adventure since I wrote: you know how the ladies
like to take control of our lives? It appears last week we left them alone
for too long, and they came up with this wild idea of putting together
a Coleman memory book. We've been told we all have to contribute.*

*I guess it's supposed to be something a little less dry than just a
family history and what days who did what, so I'm in favour of it.
Especially since Vicki (also Six Pack) has agreed to pony up a few of*

her recipes that she's been keeping under lock and key. Good food that's easy to make? Always a hit in my books.

I wanted to be sure that we get your story as well. It doesn't have to be much, but whatever you want included. Jaxi and Dare—that's Blake's wife and Jesse's wife, if you don't have your Coleman play list with you—volunteered to interview anybody who didn't want to write stuff up. If you want to do it the easy way, I can get you a phone number.

I suppose I could even help write whatever you want, although I'm not much of a word guy. Becky says the fact I've kept writing to you makes her happy, and since you haven't yet told me that you burn the letters or anything, you're stuck with me keeping in touch and keeping you up-to-date.

Which means couple of other things to mention. Becky's due date is getting closer—sort of. It's still a few months off, but damn close all the same. I'm scared shitless half the time, and the other half I feel like I'm floating about a foot off the ground. I'm so damn proud, and I barely did anything. She's feeling good, but the bigger her belly gets, the more I have to fight to keep from picking her up and acting as a bodyguard twenty-four / seven. March can't get here soon enough as far as I'm concerned. Still can't believe I'm going to be a daddy.

Last time I wrote I'd mentioned all the Whiskey Creek girls have moved away from Rocky to Heart Falls. Saw them last weekend, and they're all doing really good. Turns out the sister they found last spring is also going to stick around Heart Falls—Julia got married out of the blue the same day Karen did. Becky was trying to explain something to me about it, but it's pretty tangled as far as I can tell.

All I know for sure is when the subject of long-lost siblings came up at our family dinner last Monday, my mom told my dad that she was never missing for long enough to produce any additional Moonshine family members, and hell if she thought that he'd had time to go and plant seeds anywhere else.

Dad made some comment about never straying far from her fields, and it was a really awkward dinner conversation, which I think was partly their goal, because Dad laughed so hard.

Six Pack ranch is hosting the Boxing Day gathering. Swear they've got enough people for a full hockey team roster, and that's without putting skates on all the babies. Although I suppose I shouldn't throw stones considering how many Moonshine kidlets there will be soon, with more on the way.

My favourite part about the Christmas gathering, other than the food and the bonfire, is the snowball fight. Daniel's boys are old enough now to make great teammates. It's funny to have three teenagers wandering with the under ten-years-old club, but they don't seem to mind.

Lots of plans for the new year. I've been working with the Angel Coleman clan, dreaming up ideas of what to do with the grazing land on your parcel come the spring. Gabe is a good man to work alongside. Rafe as well, but I see him less. He and Laurel have been busy helping Auntie Dana in their spare time. Word is, she's been talking about building a house. Something about setting down new roots for a new year. I guess that makes sense. Rafe and Laurel moved in with her not long after Uncle Ben died. It seems the three of them get along fine, but I know if it were me, after nearly three years, I'd want some privacy.

Anyway, I've rambled way more than usual.

Merry Christmas to you, Uncle Mark. I never think about you without getting a smile on my face, and a lot of gratefulness in my heart. As always, thank you for being there for Becky. May this coming year give you what you truly desire.

Let me know what you decide about the history stuff. If you ever want to stop in, the door is always open.

Love from Trevor, Becky, and the bun in the oven.

MARK PUT down the letter and the card and stared into the fireplace.

Thoughts swirled—

Trevor's letters had been a taunt at the beginning, but eventually Mark had faced the truth. Even a little news from home was like air into his lungs, giving him life. Giving him hope.

Flames flickered before his gaze, slightly out of focus. So many memories came to mind. Time with his brothers, time when the SP and Whiskey Creek and Moonshine labels were just being applied to the families.

He'd left before the Angel Colemans had gotten their name—Gabriel followed by Michael was too much for the town folk to resist.

So many memories he didn't have because he couldn't stand being there watching her—

Temptation called, and Mark gave in. Pulled out his wallet and the worn photograph he kept hidden away. Every time he looked at it he felt slightly wrong. Still, there'd been no stopping his heart from wanting.

He gazed down at her picture. Blonde hair blown by the wind, staring at the camera with a shy smile curling her lips. The only woman he'd ever wanted to be his.

A new year. A new chance. *New roots—*

An old love.

It was damn time. It was *past* time.

Mark shot to his feet and looked around. There was enough to do he couldn't up and go this very minute, but fuck waiting any longer. He would take what he needed. He would give and become who *she* truly deserved.

It was going to be a wild ride, and probably take every bit of sweet talk he could manage, but by the time he was done, Mark Coleman was determined—Dana would finally be his.

❀

New York Times Bestselling Author Vivian Arend invites you to Heart Falls. These contemporary ranchers live in a tiny town in central Alberta, tucked into the rolling foothills. Enjoy the ride as they each find their happily-ever-afters.

❀

The Stones of Heart Falls
A Rancher's Heart
A Rancher's Song
A Rancher's Bride
A Rancher's Love
A Rancher's Vow

Holidays in Heart Falls
A Firefighter's Christmas Gift
A Soldier's Christmas Wish
A Hero's Christmas Hope
A Cowboy's Christmas List
A Rancher's Christmas Kiss

The Colemans of Heart Falls
The Cowgirl's Forever Love
The Cowgirl's Secret Love
The Cowgirl's Chosen Love

Heart Falls Vignette Collection
Three Weddings And A Baby

ABOUT THE AUTHOR

With over 2.5 million books sold, Vivian Arend is a *New York Times* and *USA Today* bestselling author of over 60 contemporary and paranormal romance books, including the Six Pack Ranch and Granite Lake Wolves.

Her books are all standalone reads with no cliffhangers. They're humorous yet emotional, with sexy-times and happily-ever-afters. Vivian pretty much thinks she's got the best job in the world, and she's looking forward to giving readers more HEAs. She lives in B.C. Canada with her husband of many years and a fluffy attack Shih-tzu named Luna who ignores everyone except when treats are deployed.

www.vivianarend.com